It All Happens in Γ

Foreword

Welcome back if you are a reader who enjoyed Ladie‸
encounter with us, welcome and we hope you enjoy our short fiction tales which, this time, are all based in different parts of Dorset.

It All Happens in Dorset features 25 stories. They are set in different time periods from the present day, through wartime and even as far back as the early 1800s, and some are based on actual events. We have each written a beach-themed story because that is where we enjoy spending our time. We challenged each other to write a story including the words, child, pensive, mysterious, unpleasant discovery, deserted farm and red rose and we have listed them together so you can see the very different results. Another story had to end with the sentence 'Hello, my name is John'. Once again these stories are all very different and, in fact, this idea inspired the ten-year old granddaughter of one of our group, so on this theme there are five stories. Just for luck we have added a script we co-wrote for a radio play.

We hope this book will bring back memories for those of you who know Dorset and maybe tempt others to visit this lovely county that the four of us call home.

Contents

Purbeck Breeze

By

Angie Simpkins

Eleanor hoisted the large rucksack onto her back and left the hostel that had been her home for the past year. She had not been happy in London, and since Jeff had told her that he thought "their relationship was going nowhere and it was time to move on" she had felt very lonely and finally decided to take the plunge and make changes to her life.

At Waterloo Station she bought a cup of tea and a bacon roll, which she consumed while sat on the concourse studying the departure boards. There was a train due to leave for Bournemouth in half an hour. Bournemouth is at the seaside, thought Eleanor, vaguely remembering an old railway poster she had seen at an exhibition she and Jeff had once visited, so she went to the machines and bought a one-way ticket.

The train journey gave her much time to think, but she still had no idea what her next move would be as she left Bournemouth Station. She saw a bus in the bus station, number 50, destination Swanage, "Purbeck Breezer" emblazoned on its side. There was no roof, and impulsively she climbed aboard and dragging her luggage up the stairs she found an empty seat at the back.

The bus left the town and before long Eleanor caught her first glimpse of the sea. As they travelled past tall pine trees the vista of Poole Harbour appeared, with many colourful kites as the kite-surfers enjoyed the breeze. Much to Eleanor's surprise the bus then drove aboard a chain ferry. When the bus disembarked Eleanor was amazed at the sight of the golden beach and the sand dunes at Shell Bay. The bus sped along, and with the wind through her hair Eleanor felt alive and optimistic at last. The scenery was stunning, the purple heather ablaze on the heath which was on all sides.

On arriving at Swanage, Eleanor, somewhat reluctantly, climbed off the bus. "What now?" she thought as she stood and looked around her, at the steam train hissing at the station looking as if it had come out of an old film from the 1950s or even earlier.

Hoisting her backpack on her shoulders Eleanor set off down the busy High Street. The shoppers mostly looked like tourists, browsing in gift shops, buying books perhaps to read on the beach, and children buying buckets and spades, balls, kites and other seaside paraphernalia. There were also many teashops doing a roaring trade. Eleanor was sorely tempted to go into one of them for a coffee and a sandwich, but she decided that her first priority should be somewhere to stay.

She continued down the High Street until she reached the sea. A picturesque old Victorian pier was on her right and to the left was a bay enclosing a sandy beach and backed by green, grass-covered cliffs. She turned left and found the tourist office. The lady behind the desk looked kindly at her. "That looks a heavy load, my dear," she said as Eleanor slipped the backpack off her shoulder.

"It is," replied Eleanor. "I need to find a room then I won't have to carry it around with me all the time, and my very next task will be to find a job."

"What sort of job?" asked Margaret, for Eleanor could read the name on the badge she wore. "Well, I am a nurse," said Eleanor, "but I could do with a change of career and scene, if only temporarily."

"How do you feel about hotel work? That's the sort of thing that's available in Swanage at this time of year, well any time come to think about it," said Margaret.

"I'm prepared to consider anything," answered Eleanor, "but I do need to find accommodation too."

"There's a small hotel just along the road, 'The Schooner'. They are looking for staff and they might be able to offer a room too," said Margaret. So, expressing her thanks, Eleanor once again picked up her backpack and set off along the promenade.

The Schooner was not large. It was tucked in between two larger buildings but was very quaint, with hanging baskets overflowing with geraniums and petunias, a riot of colour. The tables and chairs outside were all occupied and looked inviting.

Eleanor walked inside, the contrast between the bright sunshine and the cool, dark interior temporarily blinding her. She crossed the stone floor to the bar, behind which stood a harassed-looking man. Eleanor opened her mouth, but before she could speak he said, "Margaret has just phoned me. She's my sister. I'm really short-staffed. Take these meals out to table five, we'll discuss terms later."

Somewhat taken aback, Eleanor dropped her backpack behind the bar and did as she was asked. On her way back inside she cleared some tables. Taking the dirty dishes into the kitchen she could see behind the bar where Roger – she learned later that was his name – was pulling pints and exchanging small talk with a customer. In the kitchen a small, dark man was banging pots around and grumbling to himself.

"Who are you?" he demanded crossly on seeing Eleanor.

"I'm Eleanor," she said. "I'm just helping out."

"About time too. I'm Micky. Take these lunches to table eight," and he loaded her up with three plates full of delicious looking prawn and crab sandwiches. "Then come back and load the dishwasher." And he turned away and began chopping celery and apples.

Eleanor worked hard for the next three hours, Micky putting a mug of tea in front of her during an all too brief lull. By about 3.30 the customers were few and Roger introduced himself properly, inviting her to sit at one of the tables and putting a pile of sandwiches in front of her.

"Sorry about that, my dear," he said. "This is our busiest time of year and two members of staff decided this was the time to head off travelling. I was not pleased! Anyway, you were thrown in at the deep end. You know what it's like. Do you want the job?"

Well, actually I rather enjoyed it, thought Eleanor to herself. "I don't mind being busy," she said.

"I can certainly promise you that," laughed Roger.

"What exactly are you offering?" said Eleanor. "And I do need somewhere to stay."

"There's a small room at the top of the house, sometimes used as a store room, but it's quite a pleasant room. You are welcome to sleep there, and there is a small bathroom up there too. I can offer you bed and board plus £300 per week – it's long, unsociable hours and hard work, but you should also do well with tips."

"I'll take it," said Eleanor impulsively and with that Roger beamed his delight and lifted her bag. "Come on," he said. "I'll show you to your room."

The following month flew by. Eleanor enjoyed her job. The customers were mostly cheerful holiday makers and Roger and Micky were friendly. Micky was a superb chef and Eleanor said that if they didn't work her so hard she would have to leave before she got too fat to get through the door.

"In that case, my love, we must make sure you work hard, because we don't want to lose you," said Roger fondly. He had begun to look on her as a favourite niece, and Margaret, who visited from time to time, told Eleanor that she had become like the daughter he never had.

There were occasions when Eleanor managed a few hours off. She liked to walk up on Ballard Down, and to Old Harry Rocks. She never tired of the views. Sometimes she would ride on the steam train to Corfe Castle and walk back. There were many beautiful places to visit around Swanage.

Before she knew it autumn arrived. Most of the visitors had left, although the small hotel still had some paying guests. The seating outside was occasionally used at lunch time when the autumn weather was warm.

One quiet moment in the restaurant Eleanor said to Roger that she had enjoyed her time at The Schooner, but she felt she would soon be asked to move on as the custom got less and less.

"Well, my dear," replied Roger, "Micky and I have enjoyed working with you. We couldn't have wished for a nicer, more cheerful and willing young woman. I don't want to see you go, but you are right. I can't keep you through the winter – but you can always have a bed here, if there is a vacant one. However, I do have a booking for the end of November and I would be really grateful if you could stay until then."

"I'd be delighted," said Eleanor, so for the following weeks she continued to help in the bar and kitchen, but found she had much more free time which enabled her to travel further afield. She explored Dorchester, and the New Forest, hiring a bicycle to get about in the forest, which was amazingly beautiful in the autumn mists and equally as beautiful in the autumn sunshine. She began to walk more of the Jurassic Coast Path, and she visited

Southampton and watched the enormous cruise liners, wondering what it would be like to work on board one of them.

One evening she asked Roger about the November booking.

"It's an author," he replied. "Susan King. She's running a writing course over four days for twelve would-be authors, six of whom are residential, and the others are more local and will come every day. They will be using the breakfast room, so we have to clear away the breakfasts promptly, set out the room as Susan wants it, then serve tea and coffee mid-morning. Lunch will be served in the bar, also the evening meal."

"It sounds interesting," said Eleanor.

Susan King turned out to be young, slim, business-like and very smart, not fitting at all Eleanor's imagined picture of an author. However, she was friendly and explained to Eleanor how she wanted the room prepared, and in answer to her questions suggested that she sit in on the sessions when she had time.

Eleanor found the writing course very interesting, and even bought a notebook and began writing ideas for stories, and thinking about plots. She was a great studier of people, and had always found the difference between characters interesting. When she had been nursing she had always remarked on the difference between patients: there were those who were stoic and not demanding, while often it was those who had far less wrong with them who made the most fuss.

Susan King encouraged her to continue writing, and with more time on her hands Eleanor found she was giving this idea serious consideration.

On the final day of the course Eleanor was serving lunches when a new customer came into the bar. Eleanor very nearly dropped the tray she was holding.

"Jeff! What are you doing here?" she managed to choke.

"I've come to find you, Ellie," the handsome young man replied.

"As you can see, I'm busy," said Eleanor, recovering her composure.

"I'll just sit here and buy a pint, and a sandwich, and wait until you are free," said Jeff as Roger, summing up the situation, moved to serve him.

"Everything alright, Eleanor?" he asked, looking carefully at her.

"Yes. I'm fine, just a bit surprised," she replied, heading towards the kitchen.

Finally the would-be authors finished their lunch, and Susan King thanked them all for coming and encouraged them to continue with their writing efforts. In this she also included Eleanor. Eventually, after many goodbyes, promises to keep in touch and exchanging of phone numbers and email addresses, the bar was empty.

Eleanor helped herself to a cup of coffee and went to sit with Jeff. Roger tactfully left them to speak with each other, while busying himself with jobs that ensured he could keep a fatherly eye on her.

"Well," she said, "what are you doing here? I would not have thought a small, seaside town in Dorset in November was your cup of tea."

"No. From what I've seen of Swanage so far, it isn't," said Jeff, "except that there's a certain young woman here that I miss, and I regret what I said, and hope she'll forgive me and come back to London with me. I love you Ellie. I don't know what I was thinking of when I finished with you."

"It's not that easy," said Eleanor. "I don't know what I want, except that it's not my old life back. The summer here has been great, now the season is over I am going back home to spend Christmas with my family in Northumberland, and then I don't know. I may travel and see the world, I may even return here for another summer. How did you find me by the way?"

"I bumped into Peggy one evening, and she had your address, she told me not to tell you but she gave it to me anyway. I think she'd had a bit too much to drink."

"I won't hold it against her," said Eleanor. "You can keep in touch if you want, but my mind is made up. Goodbye Jeff, we might meet again, maybe in Swanage, maybe in a more exotic location. Who knows?"

Homecoming

By

Pam Sawyer

Gemma usually enjoyed visits home. Today, however, was different. Yesterday her boss Joe had called her into his office.

"Gem, you come from somewhere in the sticks. Dorset, I believe?"

"Yes, but not the sticks. It's a great little market town."

"Well, whatever, I want you to get down there asap, to get the info on those two murders. Did you know either of the victims?" Gemma shook her head. "Pity. Would have given you an in."

It was a lovely spring day and Gemma drove out of London down the M3 and M27 and finally into to her home county. She had heard of the deaths in Wimborne, one a young woman, married with young children, and a man, James Matthews. He had recently returned to the area from Australia to take over the running of the family farm. According to reports the two were not known to each other. Gemma pulled into the drive of her parents' house and walking to the front door she rang the bell before letting herself in.

"Hi, Mum, Dad, it's me."

Gemma kissed her mum and hugged her dad.

"Just a quick coffee, I'm afraid," Gemma said as her mother asked if she wanted something to eat. "I need to get to the scene of the crime."

"Oh dear, do you have to? It's really dreadful. Poor Mrs Mathews, I know her from the WI. Such a nice woman. She was thrilled when James said he was coming home to take over the running of the farm. She must be in a dreadful state."

"You know her, Mum, do you think she would talk to me?"

"No, and I forbid you to even try."

Gemma finished her coffee. "I'm off now, Mum. I'll be back later."

"Don't go poking your nose in where it isn't wanted and be careful. Whoever did this is still at large."

Gemma sighed. Her mother obviously didn't have a clue about the dodgy situations she encountered while working in London. Humming to herself Gemma jumped in her car and drove off towards the police station. Her old school friend Jill was a police officer. Perhaps she might give her some information she could use.

Unfortunately Jill wasn't able to tell Gemma anything more than she already knew, except for one strange thing. The bodies had been found some distance apart but their shoes were missing.

"How very odd. Do you know yet how they died?"

"Massive blow to the back of the head, but I didn't tell you that. That information will be released tomorrow."

"Thanks, Jill. I'm off to see where the bodies were found."

"Steer clear of Sergeant Cotton if you see him. He doesn't like journalists. Hey, how about meeting up for a drink, a bit of a catch up?"

"Love to. How about tomorrow evening? I have to go back to London the next day."

The field was sealed off with police tape and there were two white tents covering the spot where the victims were found. Gemma noted the tents were about 200 yards apart. A path between the tents led to the river. Gemma made notes: had they been walking to the river? Perhaps to meet up? Although it had been reported that they were not known to one another perhaps they were. Jealous husband maybe? She took a few photos of the scene and sent a text to her boss with what she knew or surmised.

Next evening Gemma got ready to meet her friend. They had decided on the pub on the edge of town as Jill didn't want to meet where she might run into colleagues or, worse still, local villains. Gemma was waiting in the bar nursing a glass of red wine. She looked at her watch several times; there was still no sign of her friend. Well, Jill, my old friend, you always used to be so punctual. After three-quarters of an hour she rang Jill's mobile. It went to voicemail. "Oh well," Gemma thought, "duty must have called." She finished her drink and left the pub. She decided she would call in to the police station tomorrow to see Jill before leaving for London.

The next morning Gemma and her mother were having breakfast when Gemma's father came in with the paper.

"You'll never guess what I have just heard. They've only gone and found another body, down by the small wood. Someone walking his dogs found it."

"That's why Jill couldn't meet me then. I thought it had to do with her job. I'm going to pop into the station before I leave. See what I can find out."

"Gemma, I really don't like your job, poking around upsetting people."

"Well, Dad, I love my job and it's not poking around as you call it. It's reporting news and keeping people informed. Who knows, it might draw someone's attention and make them come up with some vital information."

Driving away from her parents' house Gemma reached the police station, parked her car and ran up the steps. Inside she went to the reception desk. A rather sombre-faced police officer greeted her.

"Yes, madam?"

"Oh, I'm sorry to bother you but is it possible to have a word with PC Jill Bennett?"

"And what would that be about"?

"Well, we were supposed to meet last night but she didn't turn up. She didn't answer her phone either. I assumed something had cropped up at work."

"Could you take a seat for a moment please?"

Gemma looked round to the chairs against the wall and sat down. "Is he that sergeant that Jill warned me about? He looked a bit grim," Gemma thought.

A few minutes later the sergeant reappeared.

"Could you please follow me, young lady?"

Gemma was puzzled. Why didn't Jill just appear? They walked down a corridor and the officer opened a door and beckoned Gemma to go in. There was a man sitting at a desk.

"Hello, I'm Detective Inspector Rob Jones. You are a friend of Jill's?" Gemma nodded. "Please take a seat."

Gemma sat down opposite the inspector.

"What's going on? Where is Jill?"

"You were supposed to meet last evening, correct?"

"Yes, 8 o'clock in The White Horse."

"Well, I'm sorry to have to tell you that Jill died last evening. We believe she was murdered. Her body was discovered by a member of the public walking his dogs early this morning."

Gemma felt sick. "What… what happened to her?"

"At present we are linking her death to the other murders. Did Jill discuss them with you?"

Gemma hesitated for a moment. Poor Jill was dead so she wouldn't be in trouble for revealing what Jill had told her.

"Well, she did say that the others had been killed by a blow to the head and that their shoes were missing. But this information was to be made public."

"She just gave you a bit of early info then? I understand you are a junior reporter with one of the daily papers."

"Yes, my boss sent me here because it's where I grew up and Jill and I went to school together." Gemma completely lost control and burst into tears. "Take this." The inspector gave Gemma a packet of tissues. "Well, young lady, I don't think I need keep you any longer but I would appreciate you staying in the area for a few days in case I need to talk to you again."

Gemma walked out of the police station in a daze. She got in her car intending to go back to her parents. She phoned her boss and said she would have to stay for a bit longer.

"That's OK, love. Sorry about your friend but keep your eyes and ears open. We might get a story yet."

Gemma's father's words came back to her about her job. Perhaps he's got a point, she thought.

Instead of going back to her parents' house, Gemma decided to go along to the wood where Jill had been found. She parked her car and went over to where the police tape had cordoned off the area and another tent was erected at the area where the body had been discovered. What a dreadful thing to have happened in such a lovely place. Jill must have been taking a short cut to the pub, Gemma thought as she took the path to the river. As she watched a kingfisher dive into the water she heard footsteps on the path. She turned as someone stood beside her.

"Nice shoes," he said. Gemma looked down at her feet and then at the young man and she realised to her horror that she was probably looking at the face of a murderer. She heard him say in a high-pitched, squeaky voice, "Hello, my name is John."

A New Career

By

Shelagh O'Grady

"Rosie, it's been over two months now. You must decide what you want to do. The library won't hold your job forever and you need to start looking towards the future."

"Yes, I know Mum. I am starting to get my head around what happened but it's quite daunting to begin again."

"I'm sure you'll find things easier without that rotten man in your life."

Rosie sighed. "OK Mum, actually I have made a decision. I'm going to resign from the library in Chiswick and look for a job here in Wareham. If it's OK I'll stay here with you until I can find a place of my own."

"Of course you can stay here, I love your company. Now, I'll clear away these breakfast things whilst you start your letter."

Grace bustled around the kitchen putting things into the dishwasher and tidying up. Her heart felt lighter and she hoped this would be a new beginning for her daughter.

She thought back to the day when Rosie had arrived unexpectedly on her doorstep. A taxi had dropped her off with a pile of suitcases and carrier bags. Over a cup of tea and a box of tissues Grace had learnt that Rosie's fiancé, Justin, had abruptly broken their engagement and told her she had to move out. He'd met someone else and wanted *her* to move in. Rosie hadn't stopped crying for days. It had been tough on Grace seeing Rosie so distraught, but she did what she could to comfort her.

Two tearful months had passed and Grace felt it was time Rosie made some decisions and started to move forward. She was pleased Rosie was going to stay with her; she could continue to care for and spoil her daughter.

"There, I've sent an email to my boss with my resignation," said Rosie as she closed her iPad. "My life in London is over."

'That's good, Rosie. That's the first step towards getting back to normal," said Grace. "Why don't we get the bus into town, you'll need to visit the job centre and sign on. Then you can start thinking about a new career."

"I don't suppose there are many librarians' jobs in Wareham, it's only a small town," said Rosie.

"Why don't you try something different?" suggested Grace.

"I don't know what else I can do," sighed Rosie.

"Well, don't decide straight away, see what turns up."

Grace and Rosie took the bus into town and after Rosie had been to the job centre they stopped for a coffee in The Buttered Crumpet, a little café on the High Street. Grace was friends with Mrs Perkins, the owner, and asked her if she knew of any job vacancies in the town. The elderly Mrs Perkins pulled out a chair and rested her ample body at their table.

"What sort of job were you looking for?" she asked.

"I'm a librarian but I wouldn't mind trying something different," said Rosie.

"There ain't much call for a librarian in Wareham, you'd best be after going to Poole or Dorchester," said Mrs Perkins.

"I'd rather find something here in town. I'll try my hand at anything. I'm quite good at cooking if you know anyone who needs a cook."

"Are you any good at making pastry? My girl Anna, who makes all our popular pasties, is about to go on maternity leave and I need to find someone to replace her," said Mrs Perkins.

"I can make pastry, I make a mean apple pie," laughed Rosie.

"Well, if yer've a mind to, you could start tomorrow and Anna could show you what to do," said Mrs Perkins. "We could both see if we likes each other and go on from there."

"That sounds great, thank you," said Rosie.

"You might've just solved my problem," said Mrs Perkins. The three women sat chatting for a while before Grace and Rosie left to continue their day in town.

On the bus back Rosie and Grace were chatting about the day's events.

"I did brag about my pastry making, so I hope I'll be OK," said Rosie. "I feel a bit nervous about it all now. I've never done this kind of work before."

"Mrs Perkins is a kindly soul, and anyway she said Anna would show you what to do," said Grace. "Give it a try and see how you get on." The two women sat quietly, gazing out of the bus windows.

"Have you thought about getting into town tomorrow?" asked Grace. "If you don't want to use the bus your old bike is still in the shed. It needs a clean and a bit of air in the tyres but it will save you all that bus fare."

"I hadn't thought about transport but the bike sounds a good idea. I'll look at it when we get back."

Next morning, after a wobbly cycle ride, Rosie parked her bike behind the café and went in.

"Good morning, Mrs Perkins," she said brightly.

"Morning, Rosie, I'm glad you've come. I did wonder whether you might change your mind."

"Oh no, I wouldn't do that. I'm going to give it my best shot and make a new start."

"Good for you, my girl. Come along and I'll introduce you to Anna."

Mrs Perkins waddled through the café to the kitchen where a very pregnant Anna was rolling out pastry. After introducing Rosie, Mrs Perkins disappeared back into the café and left the girls together.

"Have you done any cooking before?" asked Anna.

"Only at home, but I'm willing to learn if you'll show me."

"It's not difficult, but you need to be quick. I'm finding it awkward now with my baby bump getting so big."

"How much longer have you got to go?" asked Rosie.

"Six weeks but I won't last that long. It's twins and they're likely to come early."

"So I had better learn quickly. Where do I start?" asked Rosie, putting on an apron.

Rosie followed Anna's instructions trying to remember everything she was shown. Anna was staying until the end of the week and after that Rosie would be on her own. It was a daunting thought that after just one week's training she would be responsible for producing all the pasties and homemade cakes in the café.

"My pasties are the best in Dorset," Anna told Rosie. "They win prizes in the Town Fair every year. People come from all over to try them and usually take a bagful home."

"Oh great, so no pressure then!" laughed Rosie as she weighed out the ingredients for a chocolate cake.

"Tomorrow you can make the pastry for the pasties and I'll watch you," said Anna as she stirred a large pot of pasty filling.

"OK, I'll do my best. I hope I can reach your standard and not scare off the customers," laughed Rosie. "I did rather brag about my pastry-making skills so tomorrow is crunch time."

The cycle ride home was quite hard after an exhausting day at the café but Rosie felt pleased with herself. Her head was bursting with instructions but she felt she would manage by the end of the week. Grace was heartened to see her daughter taking an interest in life again.

By Friday Rosie was getting the hang of things and feeling quite confident. During the morning Anna hadn't been feeling too good so Rosie sat her in a chair by the back door to get some fresh air.

"You should go home and rest," said Rosie, busy preparing for the lunchtime rush.

"I'll be OK," said Anna, "I just need to go to the loo." As she stood up she gave a scream and sat down again.

"What's the matter?" asked Rosie turning to look at Anna.

"It's my waters, they've just broken!"

Rosie looked at the puddle on the floor and the dribbles running down Anna's legs.

"Oh my god, the babies are on their way! I'll phone for an ambulance," said Rosie. Just then Mrs Perkins, alerted by the scream, came into the kitchen.

"Oh deary me, I'd better phone for the ambulance. Rosie, you see to Anna," she said as she waddled away.

Rosie found a mop and was cleaning the floor when Anna moaned and clutched her stomach.

"The babies, they're coming!" she gasped as a strong contraction gripped her.

Rosie stared in horror. What was she supposed to do? Her Girl Guide First Aid training hadn't covered childbirth. She flung the mop to one side and pushed the kitchen table over to the wall. Grabbing an armful of towels and tablecloths she spread them on the floor to make a mat. Carefully she helped the pain-racked Anna onto the floor and made her comfortable.

"Tell me what to do, Anna," she begged.

Between painful contractions Anna explained what needed to be done.

"I can feel a head coming. Rosie, could you have a look?" she panted.

Rosie felt terrified and totally useless not knowing what to do. Taking a deep breath she lifted Anna's skirt, and peered underneath. She couldn't believe her eyes when she saw the top of a head peeping out.

"Anna, I can see a head, it's nearly out," gasped Rosie.

"Just catch it when it comes," Anna managed to say before the next painful contraction overtook her.

At that moment Mrs Perkins waddled back into the kitchen.

"You can't have babies on my floor!" she cried. "Wait till the paramedics get here!"

"Too late!" said Rosie as a baby girl slithered out.

"Oh dear, oh dear," mumbled Mrs Perkins. She waddled back into the café as sirens and blue lights stopped outside the door. Rosie had carefully wrapped the baby in a tea towel and was wondering what else she should be doing when two paramedics entered the kitchen.

"Hi, I'm Jenny, thanks for what you've done, that's terrific. We'll take over now."

As Rosie started to stand up she felt faint and staggered. A strong pair of hands guided her to a chair. A few moments later she raised her head and looked into the most beautiful pair of chocolate brown eyes she had ever seen. Her heart flipped as he spoke in a deep, honeyed voice, "Hello, my name is John."

The Cats of Sandbanks

By

Isabel Simpkins

It was the early 1800s down Grasmere Road near Sandbanks. It was an ordinary day. The sea dark and gloomy, the sky full of poisonous fumes and everything was dirty and grimy. The only spot of colour was a ginger street cat.

She wasn't beautiful, but no homeless cat could possibly achieve *that*. She was fit, and tough, and looked like she was used to having to work, hence having a light coating of grime. But she was clever and kindly underneath.

Florence paraded the streets on a daily basis and, scavenging conversations from cats and humans alike, she pieced together the news.

It appeared that the height of fashion was now cat fur. Cats were being snatched off the streets by the skinners, as they were referred to by the cats, so they could skin them for fur, which some of the rich British bought, but most of the fur was sent to Skinners' HQ in Lower Hamworthy to be exported. So far Florence had avoided them, but she knew she couldn't keep it up much longer.

Florence figured it'd be best to keep on the move, so although her home was Grasmere Road she often walked on Alington Road. Today, though, she felt like a change of scenery, so instead she took a stroll up Haven Road. She passed a group of people and they lunged for her.

"Damn it," she thought as she fled. "Skinners!" She flew through roads and alleys, then took a sharp turning at Meriden Close, but paused – right in front of her there was a pure white cat staring at her.

"Not a street cat," thought Florence, "way too pretty for *that*."

"Paddy," he said, extending a pristine paw.

She quickly licked her messy ones, then, "Florence," she replied shaking his.

He blushed to the roots of his snow-white hair. "Who were you running from?" he asked.

"Skinners," she said darkly.

He looked puzzled.

"They kill street cats for fur."

"Oh!" he blushed again.

"What?"

"My owner supports them."

She tried to look at him with intense disliking, but found she could not quite manage it.

"Would you like to go for a walk?" he asked.

She was surprised at how embarrassed she felt.

"OK," Florence said shyly.

Florence continued to visit Meriden Close for a while, and one day even the thick pollution couldn't dampen her spirits.

"Pad! Paddy! I'm pregnant!"

"Oh *Florence*!"

"We're going to be parents, Pad!"

"D'you know how long until you'll have them?"

"About three months."

"Well then, you can give birth along the promenade. It's the safest spot."

Much later, on the promenade – "Paddy. Here's the first of our litter!"

They looked down on a ginger cat like Florence, but with white socks the same colour as Paddy. She seemed to like being in charge.

"What shall we call her, Flo?"

"Rosy," she said gazing down at Rosy fondly.

"Good name," Paddy said approvingly. "Oooh, here comes a second."

She was a double of Paddy, pure white and well groomed. She was very shy and shrank behind Rosy immediately.

"Petunia," he said softly.

The third kitten was ginger, speckled white. She was clearly the runt of the litter but still looked very naughty and cheeky.

"She's May," Paddy declared.

"Pad. Oh Pad!" there were tears streaming down Florence's face "Pad, look ..."

There, lying on the concrete, was Florence in miniature. Although this kitten was male he still seemed to have Florence's practical, kindly, clever ways.

'Gordon,' she whispered.

'Well,' Paddy said. "We'd better get back."

They all walked down Meriden Close, chattering happily, but then Paddy faltered. His owner was by the front door waiting for him.

"So, you're a daddy now, are you Paddy?" he crooned, and then he jumped at them, bringing a net down on top of them.

"I'm so sorry, Paddy. This is all my fault. I should have left you alone from the start, then none of this would have happened," Florence said miserably.

"Don't worry, Flo," Paddy said soothingly, "it would have happened anyway. My owner thinks of me as an accessory, and the housekeeper is scared of mice like me, so the kitchens are crawling with them. And we all know what lovely fur I've got."

They were just getting out of the van now and blinking rapidly in the bright sunlight.

"I know where we are!" exclaimed Florence at last. "We're down Lilliput Drive. Most cats avoid it though."

"Why's that?" asked Rosy.

"A skinner lives down here, and ..." she paused and listened to the human conversation "they're taking us down to Lower Hamworthy tomorrow to be skinned."

"What's Lower Hamworthy, Mum?" May asked.

"It's Skinners' HQ," Florence explained. "It's where skinners skin you, and they export your fur from there."

Everyone gasped.

"Sooo..." said Gordon slowly "we have until tomorrow to escape?"

All the cats looked around. They were in a cage together, made of iron bars.

"May," said Paddy tentatively, "could you possibly slip through the bars?"

The kitten's eyes glinted mischievously, "Possibly."

May squeezed through the bars, before climbing nimbly up them until she was hanging off the padlock. "What was the code?" May asked.

"300547," Petunia recited. She had an amazing memory.

May punched the numbers in. At the same time the cage door fell open and an alarm went off. The skinners raced into the room as the cats raced out of the cage.

"Come on," called Gordon, "the window's open."

But one skinner saw that they couldn't beat the cats to the window and so dived at one, killing it, taking all his anger out on it. Then he simply watched as the other cats jumped off the windowsill.

"Is everyone here?" asked Florence once they were safely down Shore Road. "Me, Paddy, Gordon, May, Rosy – Rosy, where's Petunia?"

"I... I ... not sure," Rosy stuttered.

"Rosy, ANSWER ME!" Paddy yelped.

"I ... we ... were going for the window. I thought ... thought she was ... in front ..." Rosy said lamely.

"ROS..."

"Pad, it's not Rosy's fault. Don't feel guilty Rosy," Florence said kindly.

"Let's go back and rescue her," said May.

"We can't go back to Lilliput Drive," Gordon said, "Petunia will be dead by now. We'd just kill ourselves."

"We should ..." Paddy began, but Florence interrupted. "No one can bring back the dead Paddy, not even you."

"Where will we go now?" May asked.

"Meriden Close," said Paddy.

"Grasmere Road," said Florence.

"The Promenade," said Rosy.

"But we can't go to our birth places," said Gordon, "way too obvious. No. We can go to Westminster Street. It's not far from here, and no one will think of looking there."

"Good idea," agreed Florence. "Lead the way."

So it was a family of five, not six, who sorrowfully made their way to Westminster Street.

When they got there a man saw them and beckoned them into his house. Seeing their hesitation he said, "Don't worry, I've got a cat."

So, led by Gordon, they cautiously made their way in. Gordon decided to go exploring and met a black tom-cat.

"Hello," said Gordon. "My name is Gordon."

And the tom-cat replied,

"Hello, my name is John."

The Visitor

By

Angie Simpkins

Molly sat in the chair by the window overlooking the green fields where cows grazed. In the distance she could see the sparkling sea catching the rays of the late afternoon sun which also fell on her pale skin and white hair, at least, what was left of it. She was dreaming, partly awake and partly asleep. She had enjoyed a good life, a loving husband and two wonderful daughters. "Where would I be without them," she thought.

Just then the nurse appeared in the room. "You have visitors, my dear," she said, and Molly looked up to see one of her daughters, Judith, followed by her beloved grandchildren.

"Hello, Mum," said Judith planting a kiss on Molly's forehead.

"Hello, Granny," chorused Harriet and Toby in unison.

"What a lovely surprise," said Molly, trying to sit up straighter in the chair. She did seem to slip down after a while.

"Let me help, Mum," said Judith, coming to the rescue.

"Now, tell me what you have been doing since I last saw you," Molly asked the children.

As usual, it was Harriet who answered. "Toby's joined the cubs, Granny, and I have moved from the Brownies to the Scouts. It's really exciting, next week is half term and we're going on an overnight camp. We're going to sleep in a log cabin and build a bonfire, and cook sausages on the fire, and Katie is coming too. We are in the same log cabin."

"So, are you and Katie friends again now?" asked Granny. "Last time I saw you, you had fallen out."

"Oh, that's nothing. It was Moira's fault, and she's not coming."

The chatter continued and Molly let the happy noise wash over her, sometimes managing to contribute to the discussion, until Judith announced that it was time to go.

"We mustn't tire Granny any more. Auntie Becky is coming later, and we'll be back next week, Mum," and the dear visitors left, still chattering.

Molly slipped back into her thoughts. She had been very lucky. A wilful teenager she had got in with the wrong crowd and fallen for a handsome young man who lived on the other side of town, the wealthy part. He had introduced her to the bright lights, a life full of music, parties, expensive cars, travel – life in the fast lane. She could still remember the night of the party at the large mansion with the vast garden that led down to the river. The opulent rooms with sparkling chandeliers, the luxurious furnishings and the drinks, the free-flowing drinks in the most beautiful crystal glasses. Both she and Archie had got drunk, and when the white powder had been offered they hadn't declined. That was the beginning of Archie's addiction, and from that moment on the most important thing in his life was to get the money to fund it. Molly cared for him as best she could, but without the sort of help they needed she was unable to prevent the inevitable outcome. Archie overdosed and she woke one morning to find him dead on the bathroom floor.

Several months later, still mourning him for she had loved him, and with nowhere else to go, she called at his parents' home.

The woman who answered the door took one look at Molly. "What do you want?" she said brusquely.

"I was with Archie the night he died," answered Molly. "We were together for a year. I loved him."

"I suppose you are going to tell me that he is the father of the bastard you are carrying."

"What's going on?" said a man walking into the palatial hall, and sizing up the situation immediately he invited Molly in.

"Come and sit down, my dear," and he led her into a very smart, clinical looking kitchen. "Would you like a cup of tea?"

Archie's father bore a strong resemblance to Archie, and Molly began to feel more comfortable.

Over the tea Archie's father told her to call him Arthur, but Mrs Smith always remained just that, Mrs Smith. They allowed Molly to stay with them "until the baby is born, and something more suitable can be arranged." She shouldn't have trusted them, she certainly never trusted Archie's mother. After the birth the grandparents applied for custody, claiming that Molly, "a former drug addict," was an unsuitable parent, and stating that they were in a far better position financially to bring up a child. That at least was true, and it was made very clear to Molly that she was no longer welcome in the house. She moved out and had to travel several miles away in order to find work and accommodation. One day she called at the house hoping to see her baby only to find the house deserted, and neighbours told her sympathetically that the Smiths had moved away, no one knew where.

Molly was devastated, and the following five years were still a blur, but eventually she met Will, a kind man, and they married. She had told Will about her past and he held her while she cried for her lost son. Will suggested that they move away, make a fresh start, and they moved to Bridport, a lively market town in Dorset where they had had two beautiful daughters and lived happily, becoming involved in village life and making many friends, particularly when the girls were at school, until Will died four years ago, and now it looked as if Molly herself would soon be joining him.

The nurse once again came into Molly's room. "Would you like a sandwich, my dear, and a cup of tea? There's a nice sponge cake too."

"Just a little piece, please," answered Molly. "I'm expecting Becky, my other daughter, this evening. Can you help me change my nightie and comb what's left of my hair, please?"

Once Molly was smartened up the nurse left to fetch her tea. She came back with the tea on the trolley. "You have another visitor," she said.

Molly looked behind the nurse to see a smart, middle-aged man whom Molly did not recognise, although he did somehow look familiar, reminding her of someone from another life.

"Hello, my name is John," he said.

Another Quiet Day at the Beach

By

Pam Corsie

"Here's your coffee, dear," said Maggie to her sister Pat as she came out of the beach hut, "and would you like a couple of digestives to go with it? It's very quiet here again, we are lucky this morning especially as it is so hot. I'm looking forward to the crossword and a nap in the sun."

"It's half ten in the morning and a total eclipse is on the way."

Maggie looked up at the cloudless, bright blue sky. "What do you mean?"

Pat, from the comfort of her sun lounger, nodded her head towards the beach and Maggie immediately knew what she meant. A woman whose family had set up camp on the sand in front of them was slowly bending to straighten her towel. The sun didn't disappear but most of the view of the sea did and what replaced it was not pretty, or small.

The hot weather affects people in different ways. Even Maggie, who always thought twice before revealing ancient, wobbly flesh, was sporting a swimsuit today. It did not have the built-in modesty skirt that the one belonging to the lady with the view-blocking bottom had and perhaps it should have, but it was scorching and she was past caring.

As the sun rose higher and higher in the beautiful turquoise sky, more and more families arrived at Maggie and Pat's beach.

"I don't remember seeing it this busy, ever! Where did they all come from?"

"Sheltered back gardens, I expect. You can't beat a gentle sea breeze when the temperature is this high."

Inflatables of every shape and size were being huffed and puffed into life in front of their eyes. A unicorn bounced across the sand to the sea on the left, a flamingo bobbed up and down on the water directly in front of them, an alligator to the right, a Minnie Mouse rubber ring and a floating armchair picturing a grizzly bear on its back. It was a truly spectacular menagerie performing in front of them.

The large, in every sense, family in front of them were, presumably, well aware of the strength of mass-produced 'Frozen' lilos and the like and had brought what appeared to be a double mattress wrapped in a starfish printed duvet cover. It did the job well and provided them with hours of fun trying to climb on it and falling off the other side much to their own and everyone else's amusement.

Towards mid-afternoon when most of the adults on the beach were trying to nap and only children had the energy to keep playing, a new family arrived and pitched themselves on the only remaining patch of sand large enough to accommodate them, which was right next to the Chubbies, as Pat had named them.

Apart from one young man this group of ten or more people were all enormous. They were hump-backed as the lard had started collecting on their shoulders as every other part of their bodies was already well loaded. Their bellies bounced on their knees and the girls' bottoms could have each supported a saddle. Luckily they didn't remove any clothing and two of the girls lolloped, giggling and shrieking, into the sea wearing leggings, a fantastic testament to the stretch quality of Lycra, and T-shirts that would have been baggy on anyone else but on these two looked like a second skin.

The men shed their shirts to reveal acres of hairy chests, man boobs and love handles that required a mechanical grab to go round them. Three of them charged after the girls dragging the toys they had brought with them to the beach. No lightweight inflatables for these guys. They had a sturdy looking dinghy, a two-man canoe and an old-style narrow rowing boat. Pat and Maggie watched with scarcely disguised glee as a discussion ensued about who was going in which vessel. The family were all giggling like schoolgirls as they recalled previous efforts to board.

Maggie, her sister and any others who might have been trying to doze in the afternoon sun stirred, raised themselves into a good viewing position and waited for the show to begin.

"Hold it still, hold it still," the largest of the two girls shouted as she swung a solid-looking leg in the direction of the yellow canoe. The boat must have seen her coming, panicked and lurched so it was just out of reach. She only just managed to stay upright.

"I know," she yelled confidently and straddled the canoe in knee-deep water. As she dropped like a wrecking ball into the yellow boat she lost her footing, nudged the canoe which shot forward taking her remaining leg from under her and she landed flat on her back lengthways in the canoe. She could not move.

Her friends, the crowds on the beach and even the prostrate lady herself roared with laughter, which got louder and more crazy as the men worked out that the only way to get her out of the canoe was to turn it on its side and tip her into the shallow water.

"Go in the dinghy, Babe," advised the only skinny member of their party. The obedient Babe launched herself across it, filling the space normally reserved for a teenage boy and two of his pals. Then skinny tied it to the old rowing boat.

Meanwhile, the toddler grand-daughter of the Chubbies' family had clearly had enough. She was grizzling and rubbing her eyes. Her mother swooped and lifted her up into her arms and strolled, still laughing, up the beach. "She's cream crackered, Mum," she called to fat-bottomed nan who was wedged in a camping chair laughing at the side show with the rest of them.

"Give her to her old nan. I'll give her a cuddle. Do you want your dummy, darling?"

Nan struggled to her feet to take the tired toddler from her mother then realised that the arm rests of the camping chair were clamped firmly around her view-blocking bottom and it had risen with her to embrace the child. She cursed under her breath and pushed and tugged at the vice-like grip of the arm rests like someone trying to get out of a pair of skinny jeans. Finally the chair fell, buckled and bruised, to the ground. The laughter on the beach reached fever pitch.

"No wonder fat people are always depicted as jolly," said Maggie to Pat who was wiping away tears of laughter, "such funny things happen to them."

Not to be outwitted by size or vessel the second family, the woman spread-eagled across the dinghy being towed by a large man shoehorned into the old, narrow rowing boat and the thin chap and other large lady in the yellow canoe, were laughing and paddling their way triumphantly across the gentle waves in the sun followed by the fifth member of their group who was doing his best to swim and keep up with them.

It was not to last. Just as the crowd quietened down and the tired little girl dozed peacefully on Chubby Nan's ample bosom a scream came from the two-man canoe. All eyes were drawn to the sound as the back end containing the skinny guy rose, Titanic-style, into the air and the front end with the fat lady in disappeared under water.

The big man towing his wife was roaring with laughter, his wife wallowed in the dinghy helpless with the giggles. "Look, look," a boy on the beach shouted and pointed at them, "look, look." The crowd on the beach looked and watched, clutching their sides as the laughter levels reached huge proportions, as the old, narrow rowing boat slowly filled with water and the big man sank, almost elegantly, to the sea bed.

The members of their family still on the beach were cheering and propping each other up as huge waves of laughter rolled over them. It was loud, joyous and self-perpetuating. The boy who had been swimming around the boats all this time and his bedraggled family lumbered to the shore, laughing and pulling their ill-fated mish-mash of vessels behind them. Several of the crowd on the sand stood, more cheered and all of them applauded this wonderful family who had generously shared their hilarious antics and kept everyone amused all afternoon.

"You should be in a movie," called an appreciative member of the crowd.

"You were fabulous," said another. "Who are you?"

The 25-stone-plus giant of a man flung his arms out expansively, took a bow with his still giggling family and replied,

"Hello, my name is John."

Full Circle

By

Pam Sawyer

Marianne made her way along the familiar path, although it was tarmac now, not just the dirt track it had been all those years ago. Then the path had wound through bamboo plants and it was often muddy. Now the bamboos were gone and the path was smooth leading to the row of beach huts.

It was thirty years since Marianne had last seen Andrew James. They were engaged to be married and Marianne adored him. That summer of 1964 Marianne, Andrew and their friends spent a lot of time at the beach, fishing off the pier and building fires on the shore next to Andrew's parents' beach hut. The boys would cook the fish if they were lucky enough to catch anything and eat them with blackened jacket potatoes which had been baking in the fire.

Marianne liked it best when she and Andrew had the hut to themselves. They would share a bottle of wine and make love. Then towards the end of summer and without any warning that anything was wrong between them, Andrew broke off the engagement. He had met someone else, an Australian girl, he wanted freedom and adventure, he said. They were going to travel and finally settle in Australia.

As she had dressed this morning, Lucy, her daughter, had asked how she felt.

"A bit like a cross between Christmas Eve and taking my driving test, darling. Now do I look OK? I don't want to look like mutton dressed as lamb."

"Mother, don't you know mutton is the new lamb?"

Her mother laughed. "Silly girl."

"You look lovely, Mum. Dad always liked you wearing red. He said it set off your dark hair. And don't forget your Andrew James is an old man."

"Mmm. I must admit I still remembered him as when we last met. It was a bit of a shock to see him with white hair and walking with a stick. Anyway my dark hair only looks this good because of Katy's expertise at the hairdressers and, young lady, he's not my Andrew James."

"Stop fussing, you look fine, now go."

Marianne hadn't seen Andrew since he broke off their engagement and Marianne's heart all those years ago. She was devastated but he was out of her life and she had no choice but to get over him, and carry on with her life and her job in a local boutique, which she loved. Her boss gave her free rein over dressing the windows and eventually allowed her to choose the stock. It was the 1960s, the era of the mini skirt. Marianne had her hair cut short in the style of the model Twiggy and took to wearing the shortest of skirts, showing off her long, shapely legs, much to her father's disapproval.

Marianne and her boss Mr Wells used to travel regularly to London to buy stock for the shop, which had become very successful. So successful that Mr Wells decided to open another one in Wimborne. He said he wanted it to be called Marianne's as she had put so much effort into the first place. It was an immediate success much to Marianne's delight. Travelling together to collect stock, it soon became a habit for Marianne and Edward, as he now asked her to call him, to stop on the way home and have dinner. One evening, after stopping outside Marianne's parents' home, Edward switched off the car engine and turned to her.

"My dear," he said as he turned her face towards him, leant forward and kissed her. "Marianne, I'm sorry I shouldn't have done that."

Marianne looked at him and smiled. "Yes, you should." She pulled him close, put her arms round his neck and kissed him back. A few weeks later Edward asked Marianne to marry him. They had a long and happy marriage and Edward had been delighted when their daughter Lucy came along. "My two beautiful girls," he would say when introducing them.

Marianne and Edward had been married for over 25 years when Edward sadly died after a short illness. Marianne decided it was time to retire and put both businesses up for sale. She didn't feel like carrying on without Edward.

Later that month she had a call from the agent dealing with the sale of the businesses. Someone was very interested and wanted to set up a meeting as soon as possible.

Marianne was in her small office in the Wimborne shop when Lucy, who managed the shop, informed her that a Mr James was here to see her. A tall man, tanned with white hair, stepped in.

"Hello Marianne, long time, no see."

Marianne looked astonished, not recognising him for a moment. "Andrew?"

"The very same, although everyone calls me AJ these days."

Marianne stood as Andrew or AJ stepped forward, leaning heavily on a stick.

"Well, well, girl, you look good. The years have been kind to you."

"Yes, they have," Marianne answered coolly. "Am I to understand you are interested in purchasing my businesses?"

"Yep, I am back here for good. Oz isn't the same anymore."

"Does that include your wife? Children?"

"No wife or children. Had three wives, two have passed on and the remaining one left me years ago. Your daughter outside is just how I remember you. You still married?"

"No, my husband passed away which is why I want to sell up. I don't want to carry on the business without him."

"Good to you, was he? Not a swine like me."

Marianne didn't answer. She felt tears spring in her eyes as she thought of Edward. Andrew offered to pay the asking price and the sale went through without a hitch. Business complete, a few weeks later Andrew asked Marianne if she would meet him for old times' sake. He wanted them to meet at the family beach hut. Marianne thought it strange, but why not? Perhaps Andrew was remembering his youth.

Marianne walked along the promenade to hut number 108. It looked just the same from the outside, the double doors were wide open and Andrew came out to greet her.

"Come in, my dear, you look gorgeous by the way."

Marianne looked in amazement. There was a small round table dressed with a white cloth. On it stood a vase of red roses, a bucket with a bottle of champagne and two glasses.

"Andrew, what…?"

"AJ please. I thought we should celebrate our new business arrangement somewhere where we had both been happy. Well, for me anyway. I didn't realise it at the time but I made the biggest mistake of my life when I left you."

Marianne looked confused. "Why didn't you come back to me?"

"Couldn't, I was married and working for her pa, besides I couldn't be sure you would still want me. Have a seat and I will pour you a glass of fizz. Perhaps now we're both alone we could be at least friends again."

Marianne looked around the beach hut, memories flooding back. She stood and picked up her bag.

"No, I don't think so, you have bought my businesses and that, I am afraid, is the end of it."

As she made her way back along the prom, Marianne heard a crash. She turned and saw a smashed bottle of champagne followed by a vase of roses flying out of the beach hut. As she walked, her thoughts were of Edward. He had always thought he was second best no matter how she tried to convince him.

"Edward, my love, I was so lucky when I met and married you. Poor old Andrew." She rolled her eyes. "AJ indeed."

Without looking back she giggled as she made her way to her car.

Mixed Fortunes

By

Shelagh O'Grady

"What did the solicitor say, Carol?" Mandy asked excitedly. "Have you inherited a fortune, a villa in France maybe, or a cache of jewellery? Do tell, we're dying to know!" Carol closed the front door and took off her coat. Her two flatmates, Mandy and Emma, were buzzing with excitement after she had received a letter from a solicitor indicating that she was a beneficiary in a will.

"I've got the kettle on so we can have a cup of tea whilst you tell us of your good fortune," said Emma.

With all three seated around the kitchen table grasping steaming mugs of tea, Carol told her story.

"Mr Goldberg, the solicitor, was quite matter of fact. Apparently I had a distant relative called Hector Harrington, somewhere on my dad's side of the family. I vaguely remember an eccentric person mentioned in whispers by my parents and we went to a party at his house once but I can't recall much else."

"But what did he leave you?" gasped an impatient Mandy.

"I'm just coming to that. It seems rather odd but he's left me a beach hut and some money."

"A beach hut!" exclaimed Mandy and Emma in unison.

"Where is it, somewhere in the south of France? In the Caribbean? How much money, a fortune?"

The excited questions came thick and fast.

"Hang on girls, slow down! It's nowhere near as exotic as that. It's at Hengistbury Head, on Mudeford beach, the sand spit opposite Mudeford Quay. Mr Goldberg thought it might be worth a few quid as the beach huts in that area are quite expensive. I have a picture if you'd like to see."

Mandy and Emma grabbed the small square of paper and gazed at the shabby looking building standing in an ocean of sand. Nearby were other huts of similar design, the outsides cluttered with beach paraphernalia.

"Oh, what a let-down," said Emma as she hugged her mug.

"Did you say there was some money too?" asked Mandy.

"Yes, £10,000 towards refurbishment."

"Wow!" exclaimed Emma and Mandy.

"You could do a lot of refurbishing with that wad down at the Jolly Sailor," laughed Emma.

"And end up with a massive hangover!" replied Carol.

"When are you going to have a look at your property?" asked Mandy.

"At the weekend, I think."

"Can we come too? It might be interesting," said Emma.

"Yes, of course. I don't want to play 'hunt the beach hut' on my own."

"Who was this Hector Harrington?" asked Mandy. "He sounds a dodgy character."

"I've been wondering about that. Mr Goldberg said he was on my dad's side of the family. I think he must have been Dad's step-brother. He was a bit older than Dad and from what I can gather he had a rather flamboyant lifestyle."

"This is getting interesting," said Emma. "What else do you remember about him?"

"I have a hazy memory of meeting him at one of his wild birthday parties. He owned a huge house in Bournemouth somewhere along the clifftop. I was 8 years old at the time and I remember him as a very gushing, exuberant person with long, ginger hair tied into a pony tail and wearing orange trousers, a bright green shirt and a purple sequined jacket."

"Sounds like Michael Portillo on speed!" laughed Emma.

"His friends were dressed in much the same style, the women in gaudy, flowing robes and the men in brightly coloured shirts and tight sequined trousers. I remember they all seemed to be smoking dreadful smelling cigarettes. There was a band playing and I danced with some of the guests. I don't think Mum and Dad liked it at all because after an hour we left. Dad was muttering things like "disgraceful" and "not the place we want to be seen." I made a fuss because I had been enjoying myself and didn't want to leave."

"I never saw him again and he was never mentioned. That was all the contact I had with him so why he should leave me his beach hut I can't imagine."

"Can you ask your parents about him?" asked Emma.

"Dad died of cancer several years ago, Mum has dementia and lives in a care home. I could ask her but most times she doesn't recognise me so it could be difficult," said Carol.

The following evening Carol visited her mother.

"How's Mum this evening?" asked Carol.

"Physically she is very well but mentally she lives in a world of her own," replied the care assistant.

"Poor Mum," sighed Carol. "I've something to ask her about the family so it's likely I won't get anywhere."

"Just talk to her, you never know, something may stir a memory."

"Thanks," said Carol as she sat beside her mother in the comfortable lounge.

"Hello Mum, it's Carol. How are you?"

"Carol, Carol who? I don't know anyone called Carol."

"Oh really, Mum, I'm your daughter."

"I did have a daughter but she never comes to see me."

"I visit every week. Here, I've brought you some toffees."

"My daughter used to bring toffees for me. She knows they're my favourite," said Mum as she fiddled with the bag.

"Shall I help you?"

"No, I can manage. What's your name?"

"Carol."

"That's my daughter's name. Are you my daughter?"

"Yes Mum, I'm Carol."

"I remember now. Can you undo the bag?"

"OK," said Carol as she opened the bag and handed it back. "Mum, I want to ask you about a member of the family."

"Oh yes, who?"

"Do you remember a man called Hector Harrington, dad's step-brother?"

"No, should I?"

"Well, I was hoping to find out something about him. When I was 8 we went to his birthday party which turned out to be quite a raucous affair."

"He had long, ginger hair and wore make-up," said Mum, her memory suddenly springing alive.

"That's right, only I don't remember the make-up."

"He was very odd, smoked a lot of drugs and wore the most outrageous clothes. He lived a rather Bohemian lifestyle."

"What can you tell me about him?"

"He was a bit older than your dad. Hector's father was very well off, a banker who also dabbled in the art world. He died young and left his entire fortune to Hector. All that money, it turned the boy's head and he got into all sorts of trouble. Eventually Hector bought a huge house in Bournemouth and continued his extravagant lifestyle there. He never worked, lived off his father's fortune and was always surrounded by dubious hangers on whom he called friends."

"We rarely heard from him but for some reason he invited us to his 50th birthday party, the one your father thought was such an outrageous affair."

"Yes, I remember the party," said Carol, delighted her mother had remembered so much.

"Why do you want to know about Hector?" Mum asked.

"He died a few months ago and left me something in his will."

"Hector, he remembered you?"

"Yes, he left me his beach hut."

Mum threw back her head and laughed. "He loved that beach hut; it was his retreat when the partying got too much. He'd hide out there for a week or two with whichever woman was in favour at the time."

"He wasn't married then?"

"Good lord, no! He'd ruined himself with drink and drugs. All that was left was the money and he kept that for himself. Besides, he liked young boys as much as the women."

"He sounds a shady character," said Carol.

"But interesting," said Mum as she gazed into space.

"Maybe, but why would he leave me his beach hut? I'm going to take a look at the weekend so perhaps I'll find out more then."

"Who are you? Do I know you?" asked Mum.

"Oh dear, you're off again," sighed Carol. "Thanks for the information, Mum. It was lovely to have you back for a little while. I'll be back next week."

She kissed her mum and left.

It was a cold, crisp Saturday morning when the three girls left the car park to walk along the winding path, through the trees towards the beach huts. They were accompanied by their elderly neighbour's dog, Ludo, a large black Labrador which Carol took for walks every weekend. They emerged from the trees to find a long sweeping bank of sand with the Solent on one side and Christchurch harbour on the other. A jumbled line of beach huts stretched towards the end of the spit.

"Where do we start?"

"It's somewhere near the middle, just past the café," said Carol.

"Does it have a number or a name?"

"It's called Hector's Hideaway," laughed Carol.

"Very apt," said Mandy.

The girls trudged through the soft sand whilst Ludo raced in and out of the water retrieving sticks which Carol had thrown for him. They noticed that the huts here were larger than the average ones found along the promenade. Being wider and taller they had space in the roof which was used for sleeping. With a veranda outside the glazed doors they looked like upmarket summer houses.

As they passed the café the smell of coffee and fried breakfast caught their attention.

"Let's find the hut first, we can warm up with a coffee later," said Carol.

It didn't take them long to locate the rather uncared-for hut with peeling blue paint and dirty windows.

"It needs a bit of TLC," said Emma as they climbed the short flight of wooden steps to the veranda. "Have you got the key, Carol?"

"Yes, just a minute," Carol replied as she rummaged in her bag.

The padlock was stiff and Carol wished she'd thought to bring some oil with her. After a bit of persuasion the lock yielded and the door swung open. Ludo barged his way in, eager to explore. The three girls stepped inside and looked around in amazement.

The room was festooned with purple chiffon falling from the ceiling and down the walls, gold-braided, fuchsia-coloured cushions were strewn across the bunk seats and a deep pile Persian rug covered the floor.

At the far end was a small fitted kitchen with glazed doors opening onto a decked area. A breakfast bar separating the two areas doubled as a well-stocked bar.

"Wow, a party shack!" exclaimed Emma, the first to recover.

"Ludo, come on, outside with you," said Carol as the dog began sniffing everywhere and depositing sand on the rug. She pushed him outside which gave the girls room to explore.

"Mum said he used this place as a retreat with whichever lady friend was in favour at the time," said Carol.

"It's like something from Arabian Nights," said Mandy. "Fancy spending the weekend with your boyfriend in a place like this!"

"Look, here's the ladder to the loft area, I'm going to take a look," said Emma as she climbed the short flight of steps. Mandy followed and the two girls clambered into the low-ceilinged space, having to kneel as the roof was so low. From the roof hung billowing drapes of red chiffon interspersed with strings of golden stars, tied with gold cords. A large mattress covered with a scarlet throw lay in the middle of the floor surrounded by overstuffed gold and red satin-covered cushions.

"Can you imagine nights of passion here?" whispered Emma.

"Why wasn't I invited?" said Mandy. She shuffled to the top of the stairs and called to Carol.

"Come and look up here, Carol, it's amazing!"

"OK, just a minute, I've found something," Carol replied.

"What is it?" asked Mandy.

The two girls slid down the ladder and found Carol reading a sheet of paper.

"I found this in one of the drawers, it's a letter addressed to me from Hector."

"What does it say? Can you read it out?" asked Emma and Mandy together.

"The writing is difficult to make out but here goes," said Carol.

"My dear girl,

If you are reading this I shall have left this world and you are exploring my hideaway.

My life was a lonely place; I wasn't able to make lasting relationships with anyone. They all had their eyes on my money. I admit I lived a wasted life, squandering my fortune, but it gave me some pleasure.

Maybe if I'd had a better start in life and Father's money had been kept from me until I could make proper use of it, things may have ended differently.

You want to know why I remembered you in my will. It was because you were the only person who ever thanked me for something. After my fiftieth birthday party you sent me a thank-you note which I treasured for years. Now I am remembering your kindness to me.

I'm tired of my life and have decided to end it. Writing this letter is the last thing I have to do. Now I will return home and leave this world tonight.

Farewell, Carol

Hector

The three women looked at each other and remained silent for a while.

"Did he really kill himself?" asked Emma. "What was on the death certificate?"

"I don't know. I thought he died of some old age related matter. I didn't ask."

"Perhaps we can find out," said Mandy.

"Let's go for a coffee," said Carol. "By the way, where's Ludo?"

"You turned him out earlier on," said Emma.

"I hope he hasn't got up to any mischief," said Carol as she went outside.

She couldn't understand why a crowd had gathered and were gazing at the beach hut.

"Your dog's enjoying himself under there," said one man pointing to the space beneath the veranda.

Carol leaned over the balustrade and saw Ludo had dug a large hole, and was still flinging up great volumes of sand.

"Ludo, what are you doing?" she called as she came down the steps. The dog stopped for a moment then picked up something from the hole and dropped it at her feet. Dashing back he brought her something else. Carol stared in horror as she recognised them as being a human leg bone and a skull.

"Oh my god," she gasped, "Ludo, what have you found?" She heard the crowd gasp as they too recognised Ludo's treasure.

Mandy and Emma had joined Carol and were staring at the bones.

"Ludo, good boy. Come here and sit," said Carol as she grabbed the dog's collar. "I think we had better call the police."

It was several months later before the girls were allowed back to the beach hut. The subsequent enquiry had taken a long time whilst the police dug up the whole area under the hut and found a lot more bones. Carol, Mandy and Emma had to make statements and Carol handed over Hector's letter. The media had a field day and swarmed all over the little spit of sand interviewing all and sundry.

"Did the police manage to identify anyone from those bones?" asked Mandy one day as they sat in the beach café enjoying coffee and donuts.

"Yes. Apparently Hector befriended young girls who had run away from home. He took them to the hut, entertained them and then killed them. The police managed to identify three bodies from under the veranda. No one had missed them as they were already reported missing from home."

"Poor kids, they fell into the wrong hands with Hector."

"Did Hector kill himself?" asked Emma.

"Hard to say, the death certificate said drug overdose. Whether it was deliberate or accidental we shall never know but from the tone of his letter it would appear to be deliberate."

"What are you going to do with the beach hut?" asked Mandy. "It would be a great place for parties in the summer."

"You'll have to find somewhere else I'm afraid," said Carol. "I'm selling it."

She glanced down the path towards the hut. Groups of people walking by were stopping to stare and point. There would be no peace out here for a long while.

Neighbours

By

Angie Simpkins

Susan lowered herself gently into the deckchair. "Peace at last," she said to herself. "Thank goodness that awful woman isn't here today, and her terrible children."

She sat for a while enjoying the tranquillity and the view of the bay. If she wore her glasses she could see the tall buildings in the distance across the water, and just about identify the zip-wire tower on the end of Bournemouth pier. Further along the beach were the pedalos and kayaks for hire, and in the other direction she could see Old Harry Rocks. She felt her eyes closing, and allowed herself to drift peacefully away until an awful noise caused her to wake with a start. It was the teenage children of Rose, her neighbour. There were about six of them dragging chairs and inflatable toys out of the beach hut, to the accompaniment of what Susan thought was rap music, although she didn't really know what rap music was; when it was introduced on the X Factor she always changed stations.

Susan pulled herself up out of the chair. "Can't you turn that bloody noise off?" she grumbled angrily at the youngsters, who were too absorbed in their fun to notice or to hear her.

"Language, Susan," said the woman who arrived carrying shopping bags. "Weren't you young once? Oh, of course I forgot, you've always been a miserable old bag."

"It's a shame some children don't have better parents and aren't taught manners and to respect their elders," shouted Susan in an attempt to be heard above the racket which continued. She retreated into her beach hut and began to pack the things away. "Might as well go home," she muttered to herself, "won't get any peace here now."

"That's it. You go off, you unsociable old woman. No wonder your grandchildren don't visit you. You don't know how to live and let live," said Rose, attempting, unsuccessfully in the breeze, to light a cigarette.

"Mind your own business," replied Susan, making a big show of locking up.

The sun continued to shine for the following two months, and once she knew that the autumn school term had started, Susan began to visit the beach hut during the week, but she stayed away at the weekend not wanting further confrontation with Rose or her family. Eventually the last weekend of October arrived and with it high winds and high tides. The clocks went back, and it seemed to get dark before the afternoon had ended.

The first day after half-term Susan packed her old shopping trolley and set off for the beach. Winter will soon be here, there won't be many more days nice enough to go to the beach hut, she thought, better make the most of it. The bus dropped her off a short walk away, and as she shuffled along the lane trundling the shopping trolley behind her, a battered old car passed her at speed, tooting its horn.

"Road hog," she shouted as it disappeared round the bend, but then she saw it turn into the beach car park.

"Might have guessed it would be you," grumbled Susan as she passed Rose getting out of the car.

"And good morning to you too," replied Rose.

The two women made their separate ways to the beach huts. The wind was still blowing and the waves were crashing onto the beach as they drew level with their huts.

"Oh my God!" cried Susan on seeing the damage wreaked by the storm. The roof of her hut was gone, and one of the sides. The contents were open to the elements, and some were scattered along the beach. Rose's hut next door seemed to have escaped damage completely. Susan knelt on the step of her hut, her shoulders beginning to shake. "What am I to do now?" she asked herself aloud.

"Holy shit!" blasphemed Rose, touching Susan gently on her trembling shoulders. "I came down to check on the hut today in view of the storm, but mine seems OK. There's just a shutter rattling more than usual. Your hut is on the corner, the wind must just have caught it. Come and sit in mine for a moment. I'll make us a cup of tea," and she steered Susan and her trolley into the hut, setting out a chair for her before putting the kettle on.

There was no more conversation for a while. Gradually Susan's trembling ceased and when Rose put a steaming mug of tea on the table between them Susan pulled her shopping trolley towards her and, delving into it, took out a packet of chocolate biscuits.

"Don't mind if I do," said Rose, taking one, "though I shouldn't really. My old man says I should lose a bit of this," and she patted her ample waistline. "Well, Susan. As soon as we've got this down us, we'll take a closer look at the damage."

Eventually they stepped outside. There was now just a stiff breeze, and the sun shone intermittently when the clouds parted. It was a very pleasant day, not hot but still warm.

When Susan again saw the contents of her beach hut scattered around she had to fight back the tears, but as Rose set to work gathering them together, and salvaging the wall, Susan gritted her teeth and began to help. "Look, there's the roof," said Rose, pointing a little way along the beach, "let's go and bring it back here."

They laid the roof on the floor of Susan's hut and put the wall behind it. "They should be safe enough here, unless the wind decides to blow another hoolie," said Rose. "My Malcolm will come down tonight to see what needs to be done. Don't worry, he's very good with his hands, a bit too good sometimes, how do you think I got five kids?" she cackled.

"I don't know what to say," answered Susan.

"Well, don't say anything. Let's just pack your stuff into a box or a bag, we'll store it in my hut until yours is fixed. I've got to go now, but I expect we'll be down at the weekend. Perhaps you could come then too."

"Yes, alright then," answered Susan tentatively, and after Rose had gone, she looked around her and set off back to the bus stop. Can't stay here now, she thought to herself.

On Saturday morning, not knowing quite what to expect, Susan made herself a flask of tea and a sandwich and caught the bus to the beach. When she arrived she was amazed to see a hive of industry. Rose was sitting there barking orders to a man on a ladder, who was being assisted by two teenage boys, the same boys that Susan had cursed earlier in the summer. The music was still too loud, but at least it wasn't that dreadful rap she thought.

"Hello," she said. "I can't believe it. There's a wall and the roof is back on."

"Not quite fixed yet, love," said the man speaking while holding nails between his teeth, "but won't be too long."

"You must be Malcolm," said Susan.

"Yes. This is my Malc," said Rose, "and these two reprobates are Malc 2 and Johnny. Say hello, boys."

"You are all very kind," said Susan.

After that weekend, with the onset of winter, Susan and Rose and her family didn't see much of each other, but the following summer Susan made no attempt to avoid them and didn't complain at their noise, seeing them all in a different light.

A Girl's Hero

By

Pam Corsie

"I hate you," she screamed. "You never let me do anything."

"Don't be silly, Jess," sighed James, weary already of another of his daughter's outbursts. "I'm not saying you can't go. I'm just saying I will take you and pick you up."

"I'm 14 years old, Dad."

"Exactly, 14. Not 24, not even 18. You are a child and my responsibility. I just want to make sure you are safe."

"My friends will think I'm a baby."

"Your friends won't care two hoots. Some may even be envious if they've had to catch the bus and I'm sure others will be dropped off by parents who care about them, too."

"Oh god, Dad, you are such a nerd. Who gets a lift from their parents when they are 14? Dorks, that's who. Dork, that's what they'll think I am."

"The deal is: I will give you a lift to Shell Bay at six o'clock. You will be allowed to stay with your friends until ten and then I will pick you up."

"Aaw, Dad!"

"That's the deal, take it or leave it."

Jessica stormed out of the kitchen slamming the door behind her and yelled, "I'll be ready to leave at 5.45. I'm going to be too embarrassed to have a good time, but I'd better go or they'll keep on to me like crazy at school on Monday. And it will all be your fault."

James flicked the switch on the kettle so he could make a well-earned cup of coffee. I'll have a couple of biscuits too, he thought. Better keep up the energy levels if I have to deal with Jess. She'd become something of a handful since her mother had run off with the neighbour nearly two years ago. She didn't seem to appreciate that he was doing his best to make a life for them both, under very difficult circumstances.

He wasn't the drippy, weak man she made out he was. He'd had to learn how to cook, how to iron and how to talk to a teenage girl about extremely personal, intimate, bodily functions as she grew up. OK, most dads didn't, couldn't or wouldn't know where to start with this but that didn't make him "a more girly mum than Mum," which was her latest taunt.

At 5.45 that evening James and Jess left their house, in the car, en route to the beach. James had noticed the amount of make-up Jess had slathered on her perfect skin but decided not to challenge her. He had learned to pick his battles over the last few months and this was not worth the tantrum that he knew would follow. After all, he was a man, more girly than Mum maybe, but not an aficionado on make-up.

James dropped Jess in the car park and could see her school friends waiting for her and other new arrivals. She was beautiful, innocent and grown up all at the same time and his heart fluttered nervously as she slammed the car door and flounced off with her nose in the air, as if he was just a taxi driver. He loved her with all his heart and common sense told him that before too long she would come back to him, appreciative, happy, his daughter. He silently wished her well and hoped the beach party was a success.

It was ten minutes to ten when James pulled into the beach car park. He didn't want to be late, but was concerned that being too early would be a spark to Jess's blue touch-paper.

"Spying on me, are you? Don't you trust me?" he heard her say in his head.

In reality it was, "Dad, Dad, where have you been?"

"Whaaaat?"

"Get out of the car, Dad. Quick, follow me."

James leapt from the car and chased after Jess. "Jess, what's going on?"

"Don't ask, Dad. Just keep up."

They raced, shoulder to shoulder, across the car park and onto the sand dunes at Shell Bay. He could see crowds of youngsters on the shoreline, shouting and waving. As they drew parallel to the crowd, a breathless Jess struggled to speak, so one of her friends plunged in with an explanation.

"Mr Jones, Jess says you are a fantastic swimmer. We've been waiting for you to arrive. You're much later than she thought you'd be."

"Huh?" asked James, wondering where this conversation was going.

"Leanne swum out to the buoy and now she is too scared to swim back. You need to swim out and rescue her. If she dies we will never be allowed to have a beach party again!"

"I think the repercussions may be worse than that," muttered James as he quickly removed his shoes, shirt and trousers, "for Leanne, as well as you lot."

He ran into the surf and launched himself into a huge wave. It was freezing but he didn't notice, but if he had, it wouldn't have impeded his progress. That girl, clinging to the buoy, could have been his Jess. He understood how her parents would feel, how her friends would be wracked with guilt, how their social life rested on his ability to save her!

She was screaming insanely as he neared the buoy. He was concerned that her hysteria would be the death of both of them but he gamely grabbed the buoy and put his arm under her chin and gently releasing her hands from the metal rail began his life-saving swim to the shore.

Several of the boys waiting on the shoreline waded in to waist height and took Leanne from a spent James. "Thank you, sir. Thank you," they chorused as they dragged a sobbing Leanne to the shore and wrapped her in several beach towels.

James, exhausted, crawled on hands and knees to the dry sand and flaked out on his back, gasping for breath. "Oh, Dad, you were amazing. I knew you could do it," squealed Jess as she threw herself on him and hugged his cold, wet, tired body.

He smiled, unable to speak, delighted at her adoration.

"You're my hero, Dad," she gushed, "but those boxers are pretty embarrassing," she added.

Dream Weddings

By

Pam Sawyer

As Cheryl approached the house she gave a small groan. It was enormous with large pillars at the steps to the front door. Neat lawns bordered either side of the sweeping drive, a Rolls Royce was parked at the front.

The house was situated on the edge of Poole Harbour, one of the most expensive areas in the country. 'Hmm, money,' she thought, although wealthy folk could be quite stingy and want to account for every last penny spent.

Cheryl had been running her wedding planning business for over ten years and she had come to meet a new client. She pressed the doorbell. Oh God! It played Greensleeves. The chimes finally ended and the door opened. A very fat young woman stood there in a bright pink shell-suit. Oh, please don't let this be the bride... Cheryl put on a bright smile.

'Good afternoon, I'm from Dream Weddings."

The girl beckoned her in. "Mum, Pops, it's 'er from Weddings 'R' Us." She smirked at her humour. Cheryl suppressed a shudder. With a clatter of heels on the tiled floor an equally fat woman appeared.

'Come in, come in, love, we don't stand on no ceremonies 'ere. Chardonnay, show the lady into the lounge."

Chardonnay! Can it get any worse? Cheryl was beginning to wish she was anywhere but here. They all went into an enormous room and as Cheryl looked around she couldn't believe her eyes. There were huge chandeliers, a massive marble fireplace with an arrangement of obviously plastic flowers and the most hideous bright blue leather sofas and chairs. Fold-back doors led to a large terrace with a swimming pool beyond and large lawn facing the sea with its own jetty.

A small, foxy-looking man was ensconced in one of the chairs. He got up and held his hand out to Cheryl. "Ello, darlin', Bert Macintyre, Bert to me friends, I'm sure we're going to be friends." Still holding her hand, he rolled his tongue around his lips.

"Now, Bert, stop all that."

"Keep your hair on, Elsie, just trying to make the lady feel at 'ome." He sidled closer to Cheryl. "I'm in scrap metal and a wealthy man, I want my little girl to 'ave the weddin' of 'er dreams. She's only nineteen, a bit young, I know, but I always give 'er what she wants. It will be a cash job darlin', no VAT, know what I mean?" He tapped the side of his beaky little nose. Cheryl was getting desperate. How could she get herself out of here?

Sitting in one of the awful chairs Cheryl took out her laptop and asked what they had in mind. An hour and a half later she left feeling shell-shocked.

Still it was a job and they were prepared to spend a lot of money. She wasn't quite sure how she would deal with the cash situation though. They had decided that the reception should be at The Oaks, an exclusive boutique hotel just outside of town. Cheryl was doubtful they would get a booking there; they weren't the normal clientele who frequented the place.

However, when Cheryl met James, the manager at The Oaks, he explained that during these rather difficult times beggars couldn't be choosers. With her usual diplomacy Cheryl had steered Chardonnay and her parents away from some of their rather more bizarre ideas, such as name place holders made out of bits of scrap metal. "I want folk to remember 'oo I am and 'ow I have made my dosh. Where there's muck there's brass, I believe the saying goes."

More like 'more brass than class,' Cheryl thought.

With the wedding plans well underway Cheryl arranged another meeting to finalise details. As Cheryl stood at the door she hoped this would be the last time she would have to endure the dreadful door chimes. Elsie opened the door and took Cheryl into the lounge. There was a rather pale-faced young man sitting on the sofa.

"Thought it was time you met my fiancé, Garfy." Chardonnay gave him a push. Garfy? He stood and put out his hand.

"I'm Garth, pleased to meet you, Chard has told me all about you." He shook hands and Cheryl noticed he had a limp as he returned to the sofa.

The hotel was booked, and the cars organised, although Bert was to take his daughter in the Rolls, using one of Bert's lorry drivers as a chauffeur. Cheryl had been to her usual florist and arranged for the bride's and bridesmaids' flowers, and buttonholes for the guests.

The day of the wedding dawned bright and clear. At half past two Cheryl was already at the church handing out buttonholes to the guests ready for the three o'clock ceremony. She heard the low rumble of an exhaust, and Jerome the photographer arrived in his Porsche. He opened the boot and took out his equipment.

"Darling," he swept over to Cheryl. "Well, Dearie, I must say you look a bit tense." Mwah, mwah, he air-kissed her. "Where did you find these awful people? And who is the palone in the pink satin?"

"The bride's mother. Jerome, don't be a snob and stop being so camp."

"Moi? Heaven forbid." He set up his camera and started taking photos of the arriving guests. After the ceremony Jerome insisted that the bride and groom had their picture taken on the little bridge over the stream in the church grounds. As they stood with fixed smiles Cheryl noticed three men all dressed in black appear from the other side of the bridge. Bert shot over to them, pushing bride and groom to one side.

"What do you want?" he hissed.

"You know, Bert."

"This isn't the time or place. This is my little girl's big day." The three men smirked as they looked at Chardonnay, resplendent in her enormous dress, huge blue-ribboned bow at the back. You certainly couldn't miss her 'something blue'. Garth looked on terrified. The men left and Bert came over to Cheryl.

"Business colleagues," he whispered. "Did a little job for me. Well, girlie, it's gone well so far, Garth has scrubbed up well, he used to be engaged to my secretary, but she suddenly decided she wanted to go and live in Florida. I'm a generous man, so I 'elped her so to speak, and then Garf wanted to marry my Chardonnay." Cheryl was horrified. Did these men have anything to do with Garth's limp? He hadn't really looked like a very keen bridegroom and was obviously worried by the appearance of the strangers.

Cheryl made her way to the reception to check everything was OK. It all looked fine, another couple of hours and she would be free. The speeches were a mixture of banality and vulgar references to the forthcoming honeymoon. After a couple of glasses of champagne Cheryl was feeling lightheaded. Looking at Garth and Chardonnay she suddenly had a slightly hysterical moment thinking about the wedding night. A few words of a song came to mind: 'Climb Every Mountain' from The Sound of Music. Good grief, Cheryl, it's time you left.

Saying her goodbyes she left, feeling a mixture of relief and satisfaction. Paying off the taxi she let herself into the apartment. It was a haven of peace and good taste. She took off her shoes and sank down on the sofa. Geoff, her husband, came out of the kitchen.

"Good lord, sweetheart, you look shattered." Grinning at her he said, "How about a nice chilled glass of Chardonnay?" She picked up her shoe and threw it at him. He deftly caught it. "Ooer, that'll be a no then?"

Three Men in Black

Sequel to Dream Weddings

By

Pam Sawyer

Jed sat on the back doorstep. He was cold and hungry, and he could hear the row going on between his parents.

"What's new?" he thought. "One day I'll get away from them and this place and never come back."

Jed was twelve years old and quite tall for his age, although rather skinny. He got up from the step and wandered out of the back yard and down the alley between the rows of terraced houses. At the end of the alley he crossed the road and went to the corner shop. Digging in his pockets he found some odd bits of loose change, just enough to buy a packet of crisps. Waiting to pay for the crisps he noticed a postcard:

'PAPER DELIVERY BOY NEEDED. APPLY AT COUNTER.'

"Yes, sonny?" Mr Bennett took his money for the crisps.

"Um… I'd like to apply for the paper round job."

"How old are you?"

"How old do I have to be?"

"Thirteen."

"That's lucky, that is how old I am."

"Have you got a bike?"

"No, that's why I need to earn some money, to buy a bike."

"Well, I suppose for now you could use my old trades bike. I can't promise you the job until I see how you work out. See you here tomorrow at six thirty."

"In the morning?" Jed replied.

"Of course, dimwit, how do you think folk get their morning paper?"

Jed's parents never had a daily paper except his dad bought the Racing Times. His dad's gambling was the source of many a row at home and Jed vowed never to gamble, a mug's game he thought, as his dad didn't seem to win much.

The next morning he crept out of the house having lain awake most of the night scared he wouldn't wake in time. The paper round was much harder work than Jed had imagined. He was tired all the time getting up early delivering the papers and then going to school afterwards. He had been working for about six weeks, carefully putting his money away in a box hidden in the cupboard where his clothes were. One morning he came downstairs to be confronted by his father.

"What are you up to, my lad?" Jed backed away, his dad's breath smelled of whisky.

"I… I have got a paper round, I'm saving for a bike."

"And where is this money kept, saving for a bike?" he sneered.

"Dad, I have to go. I'll be late."

Jed escaped and ran out of the door. After school he went home and up to his room. The bed was pulled out, bedclothes strewn around the room, his books flung on the bed together with the tin where he kept his money. He picked up the tin – empty.

He stood still for a moment, then sat on his bed. "The bastard," he whispered.

Next morning Jed was up and away as usual. Arriving at the shop, he asked Mr Bennett if he could keep his money for him. Mr Bennett agreed without asking why. Jed's father was well known for his gambling and violent temper.

A couple of weeks later Jed was talking to another paperboy who worked out of a newsagents in the high street. He told Jed he was leaving. Jed quickly went round to the newsagents and applied for the job. He asked Mr Bennett if he could start a bit earlier, and he agreed. Jed would rush round to his first job, collect the papers and then, hiding the bag in some bushes, he collected the second bag, delivered those and then Mr Bennett's. It was a struggle but Jed managed it. His savings soon mounted up and he bought himself a smart second-hand bicycle, which he kept in Mr Bennett's shed.

Jed kept this up until he was sixteen and left school, when he got a job labouring on a building site. He left home and rented a tiny bedsit. All Jed wanted was to accumulate cash. He worked hard and saved every penny he could. His boss appreciated Jed's reliability and his hard work. A few months later he asked Jed if he would like to be an apprentice bricklayer. Jed jumped at the chance. He had spoken to other men on the building sites and they had said he would never be out of work.

The years passed and Jed was now a director of the building company where he had started. He had met a girl called Annie; they married and had twin sons. Jed never lost his desire for making money, although he sailed quite close to the wind sometimes. He had become wealthy and built a large house by the River Stour near Wareham. He often stood by the water's edge thinking about the house he grew up in. He had a reputation as a hard man, except where Annie and his boys were concerned. He had never forgotten the harsh treatment meted out by his own father. He had never set eyes on him since leaving home all those years ago. The boys adored their dad and often 'helped' him when he was on some dodgy scheme or other.

Jed was friendly with other businessmen in the town, including Bert Macintyre who ran a scrap metal company. One morning Bert came to see him.

"I've got a small problem, Jed, wondered if you could help me out. My Chardonnay has taken to this young fella, snag is, he's engaged to Gloria who works in my office. I can deal with Gloria, I've already put it to 'er that she might like to go and live abroad, without Garth, that's the fella. She took a bit of persuading but twenty grand in cash and keeping quiet about her previous occupation will see her on her way to Florida. Now I have to get Garth to marry Chardonnay. I don't want to be involved in his... 'persuasion', I want Chardonnay to think he really wants her, which is where you come in, Jed, you and your boys. I understand you are in the 'persuading' business, I 'eard about that poor so and so from the planning office, 'ow he 'ad a nasty accident." Bert sucked in his cheeks. "I don't want Garth permanently damaged, after all 'e's got to be a good husband to my girl."

A few days later Garth Mills was walking home from the snooker club when he was confronted by three men dressed in black. He recognised the twins and realised he was in some sort of trouble. He tried to turn and escape. As he tried to run away he tripped and fell over some loose paving. The three men stood over him.

"Well, Garth my lad, looks like you're in pain. Come on boys, one of you phone for an ambulance. Bert Macintyre needs this lad fit and strong. Although he might walk with a limp."

The day of the wedding arrived and Jed still hadn't been paid for sorting young Garth. So he and his sons decided to pay a visit to the church. They arrived as the bride and groom were having their photos taken. Bert Macintyre went pale when he saw them walk towards him.

Putting his hand on Bert's arm Jed whispered, "Planning officer..."

A Tale of Dorset Folk

By

Shelagh O'Grady

"Tell us a story, Grandma, the one where you and Grandad came to live here in Canada."

It was a warm September evening in 1867 and Betsy Loveless was sitting on the farmhouse veranda from where she could see acres of green and fertile farmland stretching into the distance. She looked lovingly at her grandchildren gathered around. How safe she felt now that she and her husband, George, and their children were settled here in Siloam, near London in Ontario. Things hadn't always been this way; she and George, with their friends and neighbours, had endured the most desperate of times.

"I've already told you pieces of this story but per'aps it's time you 'eard it all," said Betsy. "It's our family history and needs to be remembered. You mustn't talk about this outside of the family; we need to keep this to ourselves. Some of the older townsfolk still regard us with suspicion."

"It all sounds very mysterious," said James, one of the grandchildren.

"Make yourselves comfortable for it's a long story." Betsy gathered her thoughts and wondered where she should begin.

"It were back in the 1830s when we lived in Tolpuddle, a pretty little village in Dorset, England. Things 'adn't been going too well what with the bad 'arvests in previous years and Grandad's wages getting less and less. He were a farm labourer working as a ploughman, a good and conscientious man. His wages had been reduced to seven shillings a week, which were hardly enough to live on, and we were getting close to starving. Grandad and some of his fellow workers had already joined a society to try and get better wages and working conditions for everyone. The situation wasn't getting any better when someone recommended they join a larger organisation, a trade union based in London.

"Grandad held meetings outside under the large sycamore tree in the centre of the village and sometimes in Thomas Standfield's cottage. He told me quite a few men come along wanting

49

to join. They were charged one shilling to join and a penny a week after that. All the men had to swear an oath on the Bible not to reveal what went on at the meetings.

"It 'ad been a cold, hard winter when on 24th February 1834 the village constable came banging on our door at 5 o'clock in the morning. He made a terrible noise and woke everyone up.

"George Loveless, I 'ave 'ere a warrant for your arrest," he says in a loud voice.

"Oh 'ave you?" says Grandad. "On what charge?"

"You and others are said to have sworn an illegal oath. I have orders to arrest you and take you to Dorchester Prison."

"Well, there were nothing Grandad could do. Being a Methodist preacher he were a peaceful man and didn't want no trouble. He went with the constable and five other men from the village, and they were taken to Dorchester.

"I were very upset and went to find who else 'ad been taken. Soon I discovered they'd arrested our James, that's Grandad's brother, as well as James Hammett, James Brine, Thomas Standfield and his son John. Along with all the other families I were very worried and afraid. What would happen to us, how would we manage with no wage coming in and children to feed?"

"Grandma, I would have helped you," came a little voice. Betsy looked down and smiled at the earnest expression on the face of a young granddaughter.

"Thank you, Hannah, I would 'ave been glad of your 'elp," replied Betsy.

"Shush, Hannah, don't interrupt," said James impatiently.

Betsy continued. "The next day our Dinniah, that's Grandad's sister who is Thomas Standfield's wife, and I went to see the constable to find out what were happening. He were a bit uncomfortable and apologetic but said it were his job to execute warrants. The men would have to stay in Dorchester Prison until their trial which was set for Monday 17th March."

"And what about the families left without a breadwinner?" Dinniah asked, for she 'ad five children and another on the way.

"I'm sorry but I can't help you there," replied the constable.

"Dinniah and I went round and spoke to the other wives. We were all very disheartened but agreed to help each other out and put on a brave face for the children. Perhaps the men wouldn't be away for too long.

"On 17th March Dinniah and I made our way to Dorchester to watch the trial. A trader going that way and seeing Dinniah's condition gave us a lift in his cart. We'd never been to the Assizes before and we felt fearful what with all the pushing and jostling in the public gallery. We were determined to support our 'usbands whatever the cost.

"The judge, Mr Justice Williams, 'ad the twelve jurors sworn in and we was dismayed to find they were all farmers, not a labourer amongst 'em. There'd been a feeling of unrest amongst the farmers of late what with the Swing riots in the area and news of the revolts in France.

Fearing their own labourers might belong to this new trade union and be incited to rise against them, we believed the jurors would not look favourably on our menfolk.

"The trial started and amongst them giving evidence were Edward Legge, a man who had often been to our 'ouse. He said that 'e and others, including the men in the dock, had sworn a secret oath. Of course, at that time it was illegal to swear secret oaths for fear that workers might band together and start riots like what they did in France. I wondered, if Edward Legge had sworn an oath, why weren't 'e up there in the dock as well? I think he were in cahoots with the squire.

"Grandad addressed the judge and I remember 'is words to this day. He said "My lord, if we violated any law it was not done intentionally. We were trying to save ourselves, our wives and families from starvation."

"I were proud of 'im standing there speaking up for us all.

"It were hot and noisy in that court room. Whilst we waited for the verdict we noticed several newspaper men in the crowd, which disturbed us a bit. Dinniah and I thought if our men were found guilty, which were quite likely with all them farmers on the jury, they might get a month in jail.

"We wasn't prepared for what happened next. Mr Justice Williams said they was all guilty and he sentenced them to be deported to the colonies in Australia for seven years! We collapsed with shock. Seven years deportation! That were a terrible punishment for such a petty crime!"

"Oh Gran, that was awful," said Suzannah, the eldest grandchild. "What did you do?"

"As the men were led away I stood up and blew Grandad a kiss. He nodded and managed a small smile. That were the last I saw of him for a long, long time."

Betsy looked at the children sat at her feet and saw their sombre faces. Although this had happened over thirty years ago, talking about it had awakened all the pain and distress as if it had happened yesterday.

"Poor Grandma," said Hannah as she gave her gran a hug.

"Thank you, Hannah," said Betsy, "that's kind of you." She continued her tale.

"With 'eavy 'earts we made our way 'ome and spoke to the other wives and mothers. It were a dreadful time for us. Anger, resentment and self-pity abounded but we resolved to stand together and help one another. Of course the next thing to consider was 'ow was we going to manage. Those with working children were a little better off than those who relied solely on their husband's wage.

"After a few weeks things got really bad, we was nearly starving, so us wives applied to Squire Frampton for parochial relief. It were a terrible feelin' to have to go beggin' for money for food but there were nothing else we could do. Imagine our shock when he refused to help! We was told he said "no person should be entitled to help if they could afford to join a trade union." He were punishing us for what our husbands had done!

"'owever, some 'elp were on the way. The Union had started a campaign to raise money for us. They sent a man down from London and he gave everyone some cash. It were such a relief! I couldn't bear to 'ear the children crying themselves to sleep because they was so hungry.

"What with the odd bits of money coming from London and support from some of the villagers we managed to keep going but it were 'ard living on charity.

"It were in the early summer that Dinniah's baby arrived and several of us wives were there to help her. It were a joyous and sad occasion; joyous because the new baby boy were 'ealthy and strong and sad because Thomas were not there.

"I received letters from Grandad from time to time. He said that conditions in the prison were not very good and it weren't 'til later that I found out just how bad things really were. All the prisoners were manacled and kept in chains. They was treated like animals with little food and water and were beaten regularly. It broke my 'eart to learn that my George was kept in conditions like these." Betsy took out her handkerchief, dabbed her eyes and blew her nose.

"But it didn't break his spirit for he wrote, "We raise the watchword, Liberty! We will, we will, we will be free!"

"It were later I learnt that Grandad's five friends had been shipped off on the slave trader *Surrey*, headed for New South Wales in Australia, but Grandad 'ad been left behind. It seems that 'e were taken ill and weren't allowed to travel. Later 'e were put on the *William Metcalfe*, which were bound for Van Diemen's land, so they was split up.

"'e wrote letters telling about the terrible conditions on the ship; of cramped living space, poor rations and beatings. How those poor men must 'ave suffered!"

"Oh Grandma, it wasn't very nice in those days," said Suzannah. "Men were so cruel to each other. I'm glad we don't live in those days."

"I don't think it's quite so bad now and conditions are getting better," said Betsy. "Now let's get back to the story.

"It were four months later that the ship arrived at Hobart Town in Van Diemen's land and those poor wretched men were sold as slaves to land owners. Grandad was lucky; he went to work for the governor Sir George Arthur. He saw that Grandad was a good worker and set him to work as a shepherd and put him in charge of the livestock. His working conditions weren't as bad as some of the transported workers; they were made to do heavy manual work laying roads.

"Back in England, the newspaper men Dinniah and me saw at the trial printed the story of what 'appened in their newspapers. News of the convictions and the unjust sentences quickly spread around the country. Huge demonstrations was organised in London and 'twas said that the authorities was shocked at how much unrest it caused. I were glad people were starting to take notice of our situation.

"We was told the trade union that Grandad and the other men joined did a lot of campaigning on their behalf. Up in Westminster the government changed the Home Secretary, and this new one weren't so friendly with Squire Frampton, so his mind weren't poisoned against our menfolk. He must have seen sense because not long after he granted a free pardon to Grandad and the others.

"That were a great relief for us all, something to celebrate! Next, of course, we wanted to know when they were coming 'ome. It seemed that it would take some time as they 'ad to stay out there for two years before they could return. We was 'appy that things were going in the right direction.

"In the meantime Grandad's work had pleased Sir Arthur so much that he asked if Grandad would like his family to join him, for us all to go and live in this Van Diemen's land. Well, I weren't so sure. It would be a long journey for me and the little 'uns and I didn't want to leave all my friends in Tolpuddle. We'd been through a lot together and we was like one big family.

"However, I didn't 'ave to make that decision; I received another letter from Grandad sayin' as how there had been a pardon and he would soon be free to come 'ome. Seems as 'ow we knew about these things before the menfolk did.

"It were in June 1837 that Grandad finally arrived back 'ome. Our James, Thomas and John Standfield and James Brine didn't get back from New South Wales until March the following year. Poor James Hammett, because 'e were sent to work so far inland, 'e couldn't get back in time to sail with the others so 'e didn't get back until two years later."

"What happened when Grandad got back home?" asked Hannah.

"We was so pleased to see him and 'e 'ad such stories to tell! The squire and some of the other farmers were not so pleased to see him back.

"When the others returned home we had a little conference. It were decided that we should leave Tolpuddle and settle in Essex. There were some bad feelings in the village and it were making it 'ard for the men to find work.

"The London Dorchester committee, the people what 'ad been looking after us when the men were away, 'ad raised some money and paid for leases on two farms in Greensted in Essex.

"So it came about that in 1838 Grandad and I and all of our children, James, that's Grandad's brother, and his wife Sarah and their children and James Brine moved into New House farm at Greensted. Thomas and Dinniah Standfield and their six children and Thomas's son John took Fenner's Farm at Higher Laver, four miles away.

"James Hammett 'adn't yet returned from Australia but 'is wife said that she weren't going to leave Tolpuddle. Arrangements were made for 'im and 'er to stay where they was. Later we 'eard that James took to doing building work and did well for 'imself.

"Life in our new homes was good. We had some 'appy times in the seven years we lived there. James Brine married Elizabeth Standfield, Thomas's daughter, and Grandad and I welcomed two more children into our family. Grandad started preaching again at the local Methodist church and he were well liked by the congregation.

"However, the local vicar didn't take to Grandad being so popular. He started poking into our past and began spreading stories about 'ow we was troublemakers and 'ow we was associated with disruption and the trade unions.

"Feelings of unrest started to circulate in our community and we was often discussing what we should be doing. The leases on the farms was coming to a close so we would soon have to make a decision.

"I don't know as who mentioned it first but we got to considering moving to Canada. It were said that the country were full of 'ope and new opportunities. I saw it as a chance to get away from the prejudices that seemed to follow us around.

"After much discussion and soul searching it were agreed that all of us would make the move to Canada. If we kept quiet about our past maybe we could leave the ghosts behind.

"In the spring of 1846 we was on a ship sailing to Canada and a new life. It were a nightmare of a journey crossing that freezing cold Atlantic Ocean. For us women and children who 'adn't travelled on the sea before, the stormy journey were terrifying.

"Grandad and I suffered a terrible tragedy on that journey. Most of us suffered with the seasickness but our little daughter Sina, she were only four years old, had it really bad. In the end it were too much for her and she lost the fight, so we had to bury her at sea. It were such a waste of 'er young life." Again Betsy fumbled for her handkerchief and blew her nose before she continued.

"We landed in America in the town of New York, then journeyed overland by train, across a lake by boat and by ox cart to the town of London in Ontario, Canada. After that long journey we'd arrived in this new land which was to be our home."

"Hooray!" shouted Hannah, jumping up and clapping her hands.

"Yes, that's 'ow we felt too. We was so happy to 'ave stopped travellin'."

"What did you do next?" asked Hannah.

"Well, we looked around and decided to settle 'ere in Siloam. With the meagre savings we scraped together whilst livin' in Essex, Grandad bought this farm and we've been 'ere ever since. The Standfields bought a farm in a village not far away so we were still close by.

"That's the story of how we came to Canada. Now, I must ask all of you not to talk about it outside the family as there are still people around who might want to stir up trouble."

"Who's stirring up trouble?" asked a big, jovial-looking man as he joined the group on the veranda.

"Hello, George dear. Has your Bible meeting finished?" asked Betsy.

"Yes, all done for today. Now, who's stirring up trouble?"

"The children asked to 'ear 'ow we came to live in Canada, so I've been telling 'em."

"Betsy, my love, we all agreed not to talk about that. We don't want the whispers to start again."

"George, I wanted them to know the true story from one who was there. We know it's a family secret and I trust the children to keep it so." Betsy looked at the children.

"I can keep a secret, Grandma," said Hannah.

"So can I, so can I," chorused the other children.

"Alright then, and mind you do," said Grandad.

'Thank you for telling us the story, Grandma. I'm glad it ended happily," said Suzannah.

'Off you go now, let me have some time with Grandma," said Grandad.

'You're not cross are you, my dear?" asked Betsy.

'No, I just worry about the ghosts rising again. But it does make sense for the grandchildren to know the truth." George knelt down and took hold of Betsy's hands. "Suzannah's right, it has ended happily for us, praise the Lord."

The Magic of a Beauty Spot

By

Pam Corsie

"Annabel's expecting us tomorrow at 10.30," announced Kim to Sam, her new husband.

"Annabel?" queried Sam. "You know she'd love you to call her Mum now we're married, don't you?"

"I find it hard to call someone that fierce, Mum, Sam. She frightens me. I know with one, piercing glance from those steely, grey eyes, that I'm using the wrong fork, wearing the wrong shoes or not making nourishing, healthy meals for her little boy."

"Oh Kim, she's a real softie, deep down. Anyway, I love frozen pizza, especially when you've remembered to cook it first."

"It would be great if I could do just one thing better than her. It would make my day."

"That's a bit unfair!"

"Is it? You know how she looks down on me and my family. Anyone would think I was from a sink estate in the back of who knows where."

"It's not really about you, or where you're from, Kim. True, she feels threatened by you. Young, beautiful, clever and, of course, you did have the good fortune to marry her favourite handsome son."

"You're her only son, Sam, Mummy's little precious darling. I suppose no one would ever have been good enough. I wonder sometimes if she'd be nicer to me if we had gone a more tried and tested route and gone out together for months, got engaged and finally married in a venue of her choice?"

"Well, I don't suppose the surprise wedding fait accompli helped. Every woman, so I believe, loves an opportunity to buy a new hat. And Mum, more than most, would have loved to have had the chance to swan about, looking her best, in front of her friends."

"Why more than most?"

"She's never quite got over Dad vanishing and re-appearing with a trophy wife and twin babies. I still find it weird that those toddlers are my half-brothers. I guess Mum's struggling to accept them and two beautiful, younger women into her extended family."

"So our surprise marriage stopped her from proving to her friends that she could still cut it with the best, I guess?"

"So the amateur psychologist in me thinks."

"Mmm, well when she rang about tomorrow and we were free, I could only say yes to her invitation to picnic at Durdle Door. I hope she packs a good picnic because I said we'd bring the wine. I thought that would be safer than me making the food. I'm not sure if it is a special occasion or not."

"Not that I am aware of, maybe she just wants to be friends."

The next morning the sun was shining, not a cloud in the sky, and the forecast was the same for the rest of the day. "Perfect for a picnic," muttered Sam from beneath the duvet.

"Perfect for a walk across the Jurassic cliffs before we eat. Ring your mum and make sure *she's* wearing the right shoes for a change," laughed Kim. She lay back, thinking of past adventures. Climbing Ben Nevis before she left school was her first, and it gave her such a buzz she went in search of more excitement. Sometimes the adrenalin rush was to raise money for charity, sometimes just because she loved the excitement. Following university, Kim took a gap year as so many students do. She spent two months trekking round Thailand, a week on the beach at the Great Barrier Reef, then six weeks working her way down the coast of Australia. She had spent four weeks touring New Zealand and was ready to settle down when Sam proposed. They'd met on their travels in Australia, linked up again in Fiji, spent four blissful weeks lazing in the sun, and had never been apart since.

Kim and Sam loaded up the car, picnic blanket, sun umbrella, wine and cooler of course and three camping chairs. Sam drove to his mum's house, the one that she'd moved to when his dad had deserted her. It was much smaller than the one Sam had grown up in and in not quite as nice an area as his childhood home. He felt his mum had not done too badly, after all the house was paid for, there was plenty of room for her and a friend who occasionally came to stay and she'd never made any financial contribution to their household. Dad was a very successful businessman backed up by a well-run home life supplied by Mum. Unfortunately, he also had a well-run work life thanks to an efficient secretary who eventually became his second wife.

Kim begrudgingly got into the back of the car so that Annabel could sit in the front with her precious son. She listened to them chatting as Sam drove the 15 or so miles to Durdle Door. I wish she was that relaxed with me, she thought. Perhaps Sam is right and she is just awkward because I married her son. Perhaps she'd be scary to anyone who married Sam, not just me in particular.

Sam parked the car in the car park and as he opened his door and stood on the grass, taking a deep breath of salty air, he heard his mother say, "Ooh, it's a bit blowy up here on the cliffs," while making futile grabs at her flimsy scarf as it flapped around her head.

"It's refreshing," said Kim as she emerged from the cramped back seat, stretching her arms in the air and pulling up through her spine. "Come on, you two, let's get this show on the road. I reckon if we walk for twenty five minutes in that direction," she said, pointing westward, "we should find an ideal picnic spot."

They set off, Kim with the rucksack containing the wine and all that she and Sam had brought, Sam with three picnic chairs in quiver style bags over one shoulder and his mum's enormous cool bag on the other and Annabel picking her way carefully across the rough ground in her designer canvas shoes.

"This looks like a pleasant spot," said Annabel, "let's set up camp here." They'd only walked a few hundred yards from the car park. "I'm glad you told me to wear flat shoes, Sam. I'd have never managed that in heels." She'd clearly walked as far as she was going to and once Sam had opened a camping chair she plonked herself in it and smoothed her hair down against the breeze.

Kim unzipped Annabel's cool bag and was astonished to find a gingham tablecloth, matching crockery, cutlery and wine glasses. Annabel arranged the food, which Kim maliciously thought came straight from M&S, even though Annabel was doing her best to pass it off as homemade. It was a bit tense. Kim balanced her plate on her lap whilst looking for a safe place for her glass of wine. Sam was enjoying the picnic but ready to put out the flames should sparks fly between Annabel and Kim.

"Lovely Pinot, darling," Annabel congratulated Sam.

"Kim chose it, Mum. She learned loads about wine working in an Ozzie vineyard."

"Oh. Good choice, Kim," said Annabel grudgingly, raising her glass and glugging back a mouthful. The food was well received and soon devoured by three people whose appetites had been enhanced by the sea air. More wine was consumed and, replete, they were relaxed and almost enjoying themselves.

Shame I'm driving, thought Sam, as he sipped at his bottled water. Mum and Kim seem to be enjoying themselves, he thought as he refilled their glasses from the second bottle. He sat and lost himself in the view. The sea sparkled and crashed on the rocks below, easily as beautiful as Fiji he thought, just not as hot.

"Oh Kim, you are awful. I can't believe you said that."

Sam spun round quickly, and saw his mother and Kim throwing their heads back, ruining the peace and quiet, with raucous laughter.

"Sam, this lovely wife of yours has a wicked sense of humour. We could have some fun together."

"Sam, did you know that Mum calls your dad's wife Katie Price and the twins are Jedward? Isn't that hilarious? They've all got the same dodgy haircut, she says."

"And Kimmy said they've probably all got the same IQ."

Was that Kim calling Annabel 'Mum', and Mum calling Kim 'Kimmy'? Amazing what a few glasses of wine and a picnic in a beautiful place could do, thought Sam as he rolled over onto the grass, staring at the sky and wondering what was worse, a wife who was in awe of his mother and fairly subdued in her presence, or this cackling pair of tipsy new best friends he now found himself saddled with?

The Discovery

By

Angie Simpkins

"Where are you, Freddy?" called Jo, beginning to feel concerned. The two children had been playing in old Farmer Wilson's fields all morning. It was a wonderful place in their eyes, there had been no farming going on for over two years, since Mr Wilson had died, and the grass was long and lush, the woods had not been managed and there were many fallen branches and an abundance of material for building a shelter. In fact they had built several, but the latest was definitely the best. It was large and, with the help of Freddy's dad last weekend, they had made it watertight.

Jo reached the river and began to walk towards the bridge. "Oh! There you are," she said suddenly spotting Freddy sitting under the bridge. "I've been calling you for ages. What's the matter, you look pale, and deep in thought, what my granddad calls "pensive?"

"I don't know," said Freddy, "look, over there, what do you think it is?" and he pointed towards a large trunk that appeared to have bumped into one of the bridge supports, causing it to be diverted from its journey down river and to be shipwrecked at the water's edge.

"Well, there's only one way to find out," said the ever practical Jo as she began to slide down the bank.

"I'm scared, Jo," said Freddy. "What if it's a body? Or even worse, part of a body?"

"You're such a wuss, Freddy," said Jo who had now reached the trunk and began to haul it onto the small strip of beach. She began to attack the locks. "I can't open it," she said as she began to climb back up the bank.

"Phew, that's a relief," said Freddy.

"You don't think we'll leave it at that, do you?" said Jo. "No, we'll go to the farmhouse and look for some tools. There must be something there we could use to prise it open."

The farmhouse was deserted and beginning to look dilapidated, weeds grew in the yard, but there was a beautiful red rose rambling over the porch and up to the bedroom windows. The children had already managed to enter the house and had explored the rooms thoroughly, so they thought their best chance of finding a tool of some kind was in one of the barns. By the time they had found what they were looking for it was late.

"I'm hungry, Jo," whined Freddy.

"OK," answered Jo. "We'll go home for tea, and then come back after or tomorrow at least."

While they sat round the table in Freddy's kitchen, his father came in and Freddy began to tell him about their discovery.

"It all sounds rather mysterious to me," said his father. "I'd better come with you. You never know, it may be an unpleasant discovery."

Although it was almost dusk when they had finished their meal Freddy's father said, "I think there's probably sufficient light for an hour, let's go straight away and look at this trunk."

With some trepidation the children followed him out of the house. Freddy heard an owl in the woods. "It's spooky," he cried, "can't we wait until the morning?"

"No," said Dad, "we'll soon be there. I expect it's nothing at all."

They scrambled down the bank again and Dad began to attack the locks of the trunk with the axe the children had collected from the barn.

"They are very rusty," he said. "I don't think they've been open for many a year."

Jo and Freddy watched with bated breath until first one, then the other lock flew open.

Dad gingerly opened the trunk. "Well, I'll be jiggered," he said, peering inside.

"What is it, Dad?" said Freddy, too nervous to join his cousin who was peering into the depths alongside his father.

"I think it's a puppet of some kind, or a ventriloquist's dummy," said his father, lifting out a very life-like small figure with a somewhat grotesque face.

"Ooh, it is spooky," said Freddy, shrinking away from the doll.

"Well, let's take it home tonight, and decide what to do about it later. It must be nearly your bedtime now, judging by the light. It will soon be dark," said Father as he wrapped the figure back up in the plastic that had protected it to some extent from the water that had seeped into the trunk.

They delivered Jo back to her home and once they got back indoors Father sat the dummy in the chair under the window, propping it up with cushions. Magnus, the large old sheepdog, began to growl, and slunk away hiding under the kitchen table.

"What's the matter, Magnus old pal?" said Dad.

"He's scared of it, Dad, I know how he feels," said Freddy, just as his mother called him to come upstairs and get into the bath. He was unusually prompt in obeying her instructions.

That night the family were awakened by Magnus barking. Dad went downstairs but, unable to see any reason for it, let Magnus outside. The dog was reluctant to come back in and Dad had to go out in his pyjamas to drag him back indoors.

In the morning, Mum went downstairs and began to prepare some breakfast. As she turned from the larder she screamed, dropping the bread. "Whatever's the matter?" cried Dad, hurrying into the kitchen.

"Look, look up there," answered Mum, pointing to the shelf above the sideboard.

"What, I can't see anything," said Dad.

"The photos. They're all muddled up," said Mum.

"What do you mean?" came from Dad.

"Well, Freddy's photo is not where it usually is. Our wedding photo should be in the middle, not at the end, and the photos of our parents have been moved too."

"You must have rearranged them when you were dusting, or something," said Dad.

That evening Dad went out after tea for his usual game of darts. When he came home Freddy was still up. "You'll never guess what I learned," said Dad. "Do you remember an entertainer called Martin the Marvel? He did magic tricks, and he was also a ventriloquist. Apparently he lived near Dorchester, and one day, I think about forty years ago, his dummy was kidnapped and a ransom of £100 was demanded for its return. That is not a huge amount, in fact it wasn't then, but Martin never paid, it was said that he was glad to see the back of Bertie, that was the name of the dummy."

"Look, Dad," shouted Freddy, "it's moved. Bertie has fallen off the chair. It happened when you said his name."

"That's nonsense," said Dad. "It's an inanimate object. It's just slipped, that's all. Now, time you were in bed."

The following morning when Mum came downstairs she found that Magnus had managed to slink into the living room and was sound asleep on the sofa. With some trepidation that she found difficult to explain she entered the kitchen. There, on the floor under the windowsill, were the fragments of the old jug she had put on the sill, the marigolds lying in a pool of water.

"Bertie, if that's who he is, has just got to go," she told Dad when he came downstairs.

"You're as daft as Freddy" said Dad. "Magnus must have done it somehow," and he slammed the door on his way out to work.

Jo came home with Freddy after school, as her mother was working the nightshift at the local hospital. When Freddy told her what had been happening she was intrigued. She went up close to the dummy and stared into its face. "Freddy, Freddy," she cried. "He winked at me."

"Are you sure?" asked Freddy.

"I know he did," said Jo. "Am I sleeping on the spare bed in your room tonight? Let's take Bertie up to bed with us. He can sit on the window seat. I want to know what happens."

In the early hours of the following morning the whole house was awakened by the children's screams. Both parents rushed into the room but both Jo and Freddy were hysterical and were unable to explain the nightmares they had both had. Dad finally agreed to remove Bertie, and the following day he drove the dummy away and left him at a charity shop in Dorchester. So, be careful what you buy if you should see a ventriloquist's dummy in a charity shop.

Beware the Creepy Crawlies

By

Pam Corsie

"Ricky, Ricky, come 'ere, quick!"

"What now? You know we're not supposed to be here. I wanna go home."

"We can't leave now. Come and see what I've found. Come on. You'll be sorry if you don't."

"Can't you just tell me what it is?"

"No."

"You're being very... mysterious. Is that the right word, Jimbo?"

"Yes it is, clever clogs, and you can solve the mystery just by coming over here."

"Alright, I'm coming."

Ricky turned round at the broken gate to the grounds of the deserted farm on the edge of Charlton Down and made his way across the weed-covered gravel yard to the crumbling stables. In the gloom he could vaguely make out the silhouette of big brother Jim leaning over a pile of something, gently shoving it with the toe of his wellington boot.

Jim leapt backwards hopping up and down and whimpering.

"What's up, Jimbo?"

"Don't come any closer," whispered Jim putting his hand in the air to fend off Ricky's progress.

"You just told me to come over here. Well, I'm here now. Let's see what it is."

"No, no, it's too horrible. It's not for the eyes of a seven-year-old."

Ricky saw red. It was bad enough being the younger brother without being reminded of it all the time. He strode forward as best he could on his little legs, pushing his ten-year-old brother to one side.

"Aaaah," Ricky screamed. "Why didn't you stop me?"

"I tried."

"What is it?"

"I'm not sure, but when I kicked it the buzzing flies got louder and louder. Whatever it is, it's covered in maggots and worms and all sorts of horrible creatures that seem to be feeding on it."

"Do you think it could be a dead horse? We are in the old stables."

"Don't be daft, even a pony would be bigger than that."

"Depends on how much has already been eaten."

"There are no bones without flesh on them, Ricky, so I don't think much has been eaten yet."

"We need to get home, Jimbo. Mum and Dad'll kill us if they find out we've been here today. We'll be grounded for the rest of our lives."

"Act naturally, we'll be OK, we usually are."

They arrived back at the cottage where they lived with Mum, Dad and baby William. The front garden gate opened to reveal Mum's prize rose garden. She'd not actually won anything at the village country fair last year but she still called it her prize rose garden. Red roses were her favourite and the flowers stood tall, climbed the pergola and threaded themselves through the hedge. Every shade of red imaginable was represented.

"Dinner is nearly ready, boys. Wash your hands and sit down. Ricky, can you get Will into his highchair, please?"

"Yes, Mum."

"Yes, Mum? No argument? No 'why me'? What have you been up to?"

"Nothing, Mum. Just going to wash my hands. I'll be right back."

"You're washing your hands without being asked more than once! You've been up to something."

Jimbo was very quiet, unusually so. After washing his hands he perched on the edge of his dad's fireside chair, staring at the glowing embers, miles away.

"What's up, Jimbo?" asked Mum. "You're looking rather pensive."

"What's pensive mean?" asked Ricky.

"Thoughtful."

"Oh, I thought it meant guilty," said Jimbo.

"Guilty? What have you got to be guilty about?" asked Mum.

"Nothing, nothing at all. I'm always getting my words mixed up."

"Are you feeling guilty about anything, Ricky?"

"Not me, Mum."

"Sit down and eat your dinner while it's hot. This conversation is not over yet. Dad's just coming up the path, when we've all finished you can explain what you're not feeling guilty about."

When little Will was safely tucked up in his cot Mum called Ricky and Jim to her and Dad and asked them to sit down and tell her what was bothering them.

"You're not in trouble," she said. "Dad and I just want to know why you are both behaving so strangely. Neither of you hardly spoke at dinner and I haven't seen a smile since you came back from playing. What happened?"

Ricky and Jim looked uncomfortably at each other and squirmed on the fireside rug. "Come on, lads, man up!" said Dad in the way that dads do when they are pretending to be on the same wavelength as their young sons. "You can tell me."

"Do you promise we're not in trouble?" asked Jim.

"I said so, didn't I?"

"Well, it was Ricky's idea."

"No, it wasn't."

"Yes, it was. He made me do it."

"Do what?" asked Mum, who was growing more impatient by the minute. "Come on, spit it out."

"We went in the barn at the deserted farm."

"Why? It's dangerous, you've been warned before."

"It was dangerous for something else, not us."

"Ricky, what's he talking about?" asked Dad, whose patience was also growing thin.

Ricky sensed that time was running out for him so he told Mum and Dad what they had found, where it was, and all about the flies and disgusting creepy crawlies that seemed to be feeding on a pile of rags. "It stank something rotten," he finished up.

By this time Jimbo, having relived the horror of it, was whimpering and sucking his thumb for comfort.

"You get these two in the bath, Mother. I'll go across to the barn and check this out. I'm sure it's nothing to worry about, boys. I'll pop in to see you before you go to sleep and let you know everything is OK."

As Dad approached the barn there was a whiff of rotting meat floating on the night air. He waved his industrial flash light in front of him and he could hear the scurrying of night animals running for safety as he crunched on the weedy gravel.

"Aah, ugh, aah," he squealed, retched and promptly vomited on the floor of the barn close to the moving pile of rags. He turned and fled. He didn't stop running until he reached his own front door.

"You're shaking and as white as a ghost!" Jim and Ricky heard their mother say as Dad raced up the stairs to the bathroom where the boys were still playing in the bath. "What on earth has happened?"

Dad was fumbling with the toothpaste, trying to squeeze it out of the tube and onto his toothbrush. His arm seemed to have a life of its own as he aimed the toothpaste and it missed the brush completely. Ricky remembered seeing Dad like this before but that was after a party when William was born and Dad smelled of beer then. Now he smelled of sick. "Have you been sick, Dad?"

"Just a little."

"Was it that stuff in the barn that made you feel sick?"

"Yes," sighed Dad as he started to clean his teeth and then wash his face.

"Will someone please explain to me what is so terrible in the barn? Or shall I go and see for myself?" said an angry sounding Mum.

"Don't go, love, please stay here. I'm going to ring the police. Get the boys out of the bath and into their pyjamas. I'm sure the coppers will want to speak to them."

Jimbo started whimpering again and stuck his thumb in his mouth. Ricky was out of the bath in a flash and dragging his pyjamas over his still wet body. "Don't worry Jimbo. I'll talk to the coppers." And he raced downstairs to find his father. Once the children were seated in front of the fire with a cup of hot chocolate and a biscuit each, Dad ushered Mum into the kitchen and out of earshot of the boys.

"Well," said Mum. "What is going on?"

"I've told the law what the boys found and what I saw in the barn. They should be here any minute, they'll want to interview Ricky and Jim."

"Why, what did they find?"

"Who did they find would be a better question."

"It was a person? They found a person in the barn!"

"I'm sure they don't realise. They don't seem that worried. Jimbo is a bit upset but I think that's more because he thinks he will be in trouble. Ricky couldn't be more excited. It was horrible. The rank smell, the flies and maggots feasting on the poor lad. I'm afraid I lost the plot a bit and just ran once I stopped being sick."

"Poor lad? Who was it? Someone we know? Did you recognise him?"

"No, I didn't recognise him. I thought he was youngish, he was wearing a hoodie and tracksuit bottoms and he had one trainer on and another was nearby. Of course, it was all filthy and difficult to identify."

The doorbell rang and the boys yelled for Dad to answer the door. Dad led PCs Roberts and James from the Dorset Police Force into the lounge. Jim was snuggled up half behind Ricky who was sitting up straight looking brave but Dad noticed that his knuckles were white where he gripped the arm of the sofa.

"Hello, lads. I'm PC Roberts, you can call me Robbie if you like, everybody does."

"Hello, Robbie," they whispered.

"I'm just going to have a chat with your mum and dad in the kitchen then I'll be back to ask you two a few questions about what you have discovered in the barn."

Jimbo and Ricky were left on the sofa finishing their hot chocolate with PC James, also known as Jimbo. As the adults entered the kitchen Robbie pulled the door shut and in an exaggerated whisper said, "They don't seem very upset so I'm guessing they don't realise they found the remains of the Head Boy at the village school. He's been missing for more than a week. We'll have to have a post mortem but Sarge is pretty confident."

"Oh, no. Not Andrew," whispered Mum. "He was such a nice boy. I'm a dinner lady at the school three days a week. I know him quite well. He was always so polite, so cheerful."

"He was also supplying weed to half the sixth form," said Robbie. "Not all his contacts were people you'd want your kids to be friends with. We're not to make judgments without evidence or a post mortem, but you mark my words. He was a wrong 'un and it looks like his supplier may have caught up with him."

"Ooh," whispered Mum grabbing at her husband's arm. "I think I'm going to faint," and she slumped to the floor. At the sound of her hitting the deck Ricky and Jimbo charged through the door.

"Oh no," cried Jimbo launching himself over his mother's prostrate body. "Get up Mum, don't let the creepy crawlies get you like that man in the barn."

"Kids," said Robbie, "don't miss a thing, do they?"

Summer Holidays in Dorset

By

Shelagh O'Grady

"Come on, I'll race you to the beach," Sam called to his younger sister as he took off along the sandy path.

"Wait for me," called Abbie, struggling with buckets and spades.

Sam and Abbie, 11 and 9 years old, were staying with their grandparents for their school summer break. Their parents would be coming down from London in two weeks' time to join in the fun.

Nanny and Grampy lived in one of several old fishermen's cottages nestling in a secluded cove on the Dorset coast. Years ago there had been a thriving fishing industry but now with bigger boats the trade had moved to Poole. The road to the small huddle of cottages was narrow and twisty and few visitors tackled the awkward road. Grampy's house was nearest to the beach, just behind the grassy sand dunes, and the children loved to run down to the beach every day.

Arriving on the sand, Abbie dropped the buckets and spades and joined her brother paddling in the surf. A stiff breeze was making big waves with lots of spray.

"Help me build a castle, Sam," said Abbie.

"Yeah, alright then," Sam replied with little enthusiasm. He grabbed a spade and made a start. Soon they had a huge pile of sand and Abbie started to shape it into a castle with turrets, whilst Sam wandered off along the beach. Picking up handfuls of shells, Abbie decorated the castle and made it pretty. She looked along the beach to find Sam and saw him coming back dragging a huge piece of seaweed.

"Come and look at the castle," she called as Sam approached.

"Yeah, not bad," he said. "It will look even better with this on top of it." He laughed as he swung the huge piece of seaweed and dumped it on top of the castle, damaging all of Abbie's hard work.

"Sam, that's not fair," she cried as she charged towards him. Sam dodged his angry sister and ran off down the beach with Abbie chasing after him threatening all manner of retribution. They splashed through the surf and jumped over piles of seaweed until at last Sam threw himself onto the sand. Abbie caught up and dropped a load of wet seaweed over his head.

"That's for ruining the castle," she laughed, her annoyance having evaporated. Sam picked the wet seaweed off his face and sat up. They were nearly at the rocky outcrop which marked the end of the cove and he realised they hadn't ventured this far along the beach before. He saw a little path through the sand dunes and what looked like a wood further on.

"Let's go and explore," he said. "Come on, we'll see where that path goes."

They climbed through the grassy sand dunes and at the top of the bank found a copse of scrubby, weather beaten-trees, twisted by the wind into weird shapes. The path, now little more than a rabbit run, continued through the trees.

"Let's see where it goes," said Sam, excitedly.

They picked their way past the twisted branches and stepped carefully over prickly bramble stems.

"This is creepy," said Abbie.

"Not frightened of a tree are you?" asked Sam.

"No, course not," replied Abbie. "It's just the weird shapes they make."

Presently they saw some derelict farm buildings. The farm yard was overgrown with weeds, the front door sagged open and many of the windows were broken. The roofs on the outhouses had caved in with tiles hanging at crazy angles.

"Let's have a look inside," suggested Sam.

"It's a bit creepy," said Abbie hesitantly.

"It's just old and rotten. Be careful where you walk."

The children pushed past the sagging door which squeaked loudly and found themselves in the kitchen. Through a broken window a rose bush had thrust its branches and red roses bloomed amongst the cobwebs. A dresser full of pretty plates stood against one wall and an old fashioned stone sink stood against the other. Everywhere was covered in dirt and dead leaves.

"It smells funny in here," said Abbie wrinkling her nose.

"That's 'cos it's old and rotten," said Sam. The two children peered around the dimly lit room and Sam noticed a new looking sports holdall on a chair beside the range.

"Look, a sports bag like Dad's. I wonder who left that here," said Sam as he unzipped it and looked inside. "Cor blimey," he exclaimed in his strong cockney accent, "just take a look at this!" He pulled out two iPads, several smartphones and was starting to lift out some jewellery when Abbie joined him.

"Let me have a look," she said excitedly. She put her hand in and grabbed a string of pearls. "These are pretty beads," she said as she hung them round her neck. Next she pulled out a diamond necklace, the stones glinting in the pale light. As she had difficulty undoing the clasp she put it on her head like a tiara.

"Who does all this belong to?" she asked as she slid some gold bangles onto her wrists. "No one lives here."

"I don't know. Someone must have left it here and forgotten about it," said Sam as he pulled a large wad of £50 notes from the bag.

"I wouldn't forget about these pretty necklaces," said Abbie as she looped a heavy gold chain around her neck. "Do I look beautiful, Sam?" she asked.

"Put them back, they're not yours," he said. "I'm going to have a look around the rest of the place."

"I'm coming too," said Abbie. Standing up she resembled a display stand in a jeweller's window.

Sam opened a door leading from the kitchen and immediately both children started choking on the terrible smell pouring from the room. Hordes of big black flies buzzed past them and Abbie screamed.

"This is horrid!" she shouted. "Let's get out." Both children ran from the house coughing madly, glad to breathe the fresh seaside air.

"What's in there making that smell?" asked Abbie. "And why are all those flies in there?"

"Do you remember when Mum was out and we watched that horror film with all those dead bodies?" asked Sam.

"Yes," replied Abbie.

"Well..." Sam began.

"A dead body, in there?" gasped Abbie.

"Well, maybe," said Sam. "I'm going back to have another look. It might just be a dead animal. You can stay here if you don't want to come."

"No, don't leave me here, I'm coming too," she said.

The two children returned to the house and standing at the door to the back room peered inside. The smell was as strong as ever, catching in their throats, and there were just as many flies buzzing around. By the dim light coming through a filthy net curtain they could see a mound on a bed under the window. Abbie waited by the door as Sam went to look.

"What is it?" Abbie asked in a whisper.

Sam retched and then vomited before he turned and ran for the door. Outside in the garden he sat on a log and gasped for air, his face deathly pale.

"Are you OK Sam?" asked Abbie. "What was it?"

"It was horrible, Abbie, worse than that film, and all those flies, ugh!"

"But what was it?" demanded Abbie itching to know.

"I think it was a man but he was dead. His body was all blown up and the flies were crawling over his face; in his mouth, up his nose and all over his eyes. It was awful! I couldn't help being sick."

"Let's go home, I don't like it here anymore," said Abbie, tears welling up into her eyes.

"Come on, let's tell Grampy, he'll know what to do," said Sam.

The children started back along the path and ran as fast as they could along the sand. Before they reached Grampy's house they met him anxiously searching the beach.

"Where have you been?" asked a worried Grampy. "It's way past lunch time. Nanna sent me to look for you." Seeing the necklaces around Abbie's neck he asked, "Where did you get that jewellery, Abbie?" Between gasps the children told their tale as they walked to the cottage.

Grampy rang the local police station as the children ate their lunch. Later that afternoon PC Graham Eaton from Dorset Police arrived and listened to the children's story, writing everything in his notebook.

"We'll send someone to check out that old farm. It hasn't been occupied for a long time so maybe unpleasant things have happened there. I'll have to take those pretty necklaces from you, my dear," he said to Abbie, "and that wad of cash from you Sam." The children reluctantly handed over their findings

"They will be locked in a safe at the police station in Dorchester until we can find their rightful owners."

It was some months later when Sam and Abbie were visiting Nanna and Grampy's for Halloween that PC Eaton called again. Sitting in the lounge they were eager to hear what he had to say.

"I expect you'd like to know what we found out about the old farm," he began.

"Oh, yes please," cried Sam and Abbie.

"Well, it seems that a gang of thieves had been robbing big houses in this area. One night they had an argument and a fight broke out. The man you found had shot his mate and run away from the others, taking a bag of stolen goods with him. Unfortunately he had a stab wound to his stomach, so had hidden in the old farm house to recover, but he died. It was a couple of weeks later that you two found him."

"He smelt terrible," said Abbie, pulling a face at the memory.

"I have some good news for you," announced the policeman. "Some of the stolen property belonged to one of the local land owners and they were very pleased to get it back. When they heard the story of how the two of you found the bag of stolen property along with the unpleasant dead body they decided to give you a reward." PC Eaton took a large envelope from his bag and handed it to Sam. "I think this will please you both," he said.

Whilst Abbie watched, Sam tore open the envelope and pulled out a brightly coloured brochure. "It's tickets to visit Euro Disney in Paris for you and your family," said PC Eaton.

"Whoopee, we're going to Euro Disney! Yeah," Sam shouted as he jumped up and down.

"Let me see! I want to see!" shouted Abbie trying to grab the brochure from Sam.

"That was very generous," said Grampy. "It will give the whole family a chance to enjoy themselves together."

"We'll need to thank these people," said Nanna.

"Just drop them a note, that's all that's needed," said PC Eaton. "The owners were very relieved to have some irreplaceable items returned, thanks to Sam and Abbie."

PC Eaton left the cottage feeling great; delivering good news was the part of his job he liked the best.

Fresh Fields

By

Pam Sawyer

Anna pulled into the gateway just as the disembodied voice from the sat nav in the hire car told her she had reached her destination. Opening the door, Anna stepped out of the car into bright sunshine and walked to the gate. There was a sign on the gate.

'Hmm, Home Farm,' she read. "Doesn't look much like a home." Opening the gate she walked up the short path to the farmhouse door. Anna stopped and looked around. The silence was almost deafening, only now and again interrupted by the sound of a bird chirping in the nearby hedge.

She could hardly believe the speed at which her life had changed. A few weeks ago living in an apartment in New York with Pete, her husband, she thought that's how her life would pan out, living in the city she loved, brash, noisy, sometimes scary. Then the bombshell. Pete asked her for a divorce. He said now their two daughters had virtually left home he felt trapped in their marriage and wanted his freedom. Anna was stunned. Bonnie, their eldest daughter, had finished college and had gone travelling. Roseanne, the youngest, was in the UK. She had gained a place at Imperial College London.

More shocks were to come for Anna. A week after Pete had said their marriage was over she received a letter from a firm of solicitors in London. She was the sole surviving relative of a George Adams. Anna had never heard of him but apparently she had inherited a farm in England in a village called Toller Porcorum in Dorset. At first Anna thought it was a joke. She checked on the internet and found there was such a place. Now here she was standing at the front door of her property.

The key turned easily in the lock as Anna let herself into a dark hall. Looking around, she tried the first door nearest to her. It opened into an equally gloomy kitchen. Standing by the sink looking out of the window at the deserted farm, Anna's first thought was, "Sell it, that's what would be best, and go back to the US." After all that was where her life was, with or without Pete.

Anna left the kitchen and went into what was the living room. She saw a threadbare carpet, an old sagging sofa in front of an inglenook fireplace and a bureau. The walls were brown and, in places, a lighter colour where it looked as though furniture had stood until recently. How mysterious, Anna thought, who could have taken it? Looking around at other bits and pieces she doubted there had been anything of value in this room. Making her way upstairs she stopped on the landing and looked down on the empty farm yard. Suddenly a black cat raced from under the dilapidated door of the nearby barn, and the door was pushed open and a man appeared. He didn't look up so, obviously, didn't know Anna had seen him.

"Oh my goodness, who are you?" Suddenly Anna felt scared as he went round to the front of the house. He was bound to see her car and she realised she hadn't locked the front door behind her. "Pull yourself together, woman, this is rural England not New York," she muttered to herself. Although she still felt uneasy.

Her fears were realised when she heard footsteps on the stairs. She opened the nearest door, an empty room apart from a single bed with a bare mattress. She stood behind the door her heart thumping. Then she heard another door open and close. Creeping out of the room Anna reached the top of the stairs when an arm grabbed her around the throat. She tried to scream but his grip was too tight.

"Who the bloody hell are you?" the man said as he loosened his grip slightly.

"Let me go!" Anna's voice was hoarse as she tried to struggle free but he was too strong and tightened his grip again. Anna let herself relax and her attacker loosened his grip. "I'll ask you again, who are you and what are you doing here?" Anna quickly wriggled round and kneed him in the groin. He let go of her and fell to his knees. Anna started down the stairs. Nearing the bottom of the stairs she tripped and felt a bolt of pain shoot up her leg. Crying with pain she saw that the man had recovered and was making his way down the stairs.

"Please don't hurt me," she cried as he loomed over her.

"If you had told me who you are in the first place neither of us would have been hurt. Now let me look at your leg while you tell me who you are and what you are doing here."

"My name is Anna Hutchison. I have just arrived from New York to come and look over this property which has been left to me."

"I'm sorry, we seem to have got off on the wrong foot. Oh dear, 'scuse the pun. Let me introduce myself, Mrs Hutchison. I am a police officer with the Dorset Police, DS James Walker." He knelt beside her and gently examined her leg. "Probably just a sprain but I think we should get it looked at."

"You're a cop? Well, what are you doing creeping up on folk and nearly strangling them?"

"There have been quite a lot of goings on at this farm since Mr Adams passed away six months ago. Youngsters getting in the barn drinking and taking drugs."

"Drinking? Drugs? I thought this was a quiet country place. Sounds more like New York."

"Well, I can't comment on that, never been there. But a week ago some lads were in the barn when one of them decided to climb up to the hayloft. He fell through the old floor. Fortunately he wasn't badly hurt. When his mates picked him up they made an unpleasant discovery. The lad had made a grab at a rope to try and save himself. The rope was tied around a sack and when they opened it they found some bones which looked like the remains of a baby."

"Good grief. How long had it been there?"

"Well, we're waiting for forensics to give us some idea. Now my car is parked around the back of the barn, let's lock up here and get you to A&E to look at that leg." Anna looked at the officer properly for the first time. He was tall, dark-haired and quite good looking. He smiled at her. "Right, I'll just get the car then." Anna gave him her house and car keys and he went off to fetch his car to the front of the house. He was soon back and gently helped Anna to her feet although she couldn't put her injured leg to the floor.

"OK, I'll have to carry you." He scooped Anna up and went with her to his car. It was a bit of a struggle to get her in but soon she was seated and belted while he went to lock the house and Anna's hire car. As they drove off Anna said, "You know I could sue for what you have done to me."

"Try it lady, I didn't push you, you tripped and fell. Clumsy, I'd call it. I was checking out what could have been an intruder. Doing my duty, so I don't think we need to hear any more of suing do we? Or I might arrest you for your attack on me." He looked in the rear view mirror and saw the beginnings of a smile on her face.

On arriving at the hospital in Dorchester, Anna was seen promptly when James Walker flashed his warrant card. She was checked over and her leg X-rayed.

"No broken bones, my dear," the doctor said when her results returned. "Just a nasty sprain. You will need to rest it and use a stick when walking. Is there anyone I can contact for you?"

"No," Anna looked pensive. "Thank you." No good contacting Pete, she thought.

"It's OK, Doctor, I'll sort Mrs Hutchison out, take her back to her B&B and get her hire car collected." With that he helped Anna into a wheelchair, collected a walking stick and some painkillers and took her out to his car.

"I cannot believe this has happened. I am due to fly back home at the end of the week."

"Well, we will have to see how things go, won't we? Now, you said you were staying at Mrs Tyler's next to the Post Office in the village, that right?"

"Yes, but how can you do this for me? Aren't you on duty or something?"

"I am. I was dealing with an intruder, remember?"

Anna chuckled. She was beginning to like DS James Walker.

The next morning Anna received a text from Pete. He had received a very good offer on their apartment and wanted to know if she would go with it. He realised she might be delayed in getting back to New York after her accident but they could sort details later. Anna had mixed feelings when she read the text. She had been thinking about her and Pete's relationship and how things had changed between them. He was always out, either at his office or his spare time was taken with the baseball team he was helping to coach. She loved the apartment with its view of the Hudson River but she realised she would rattle around there alone most of the time now both girls had left.

The next day Mrs Tyler offered to take Anna back to the farm. She seemed quite keen to go with Anna, her curiosity aroused about the grim findings. The barn was sealed off with police tape but they were able to look around the house and garden. Anna couldn't manage the stairs but she was looking at the building with new light. It was built with brick and flint, DS Walker had told her, and looked pretty in the morning sunshine.

Leaving Mrs Tyler to wander upstairs Anna hobbled with her stick to the rear of the property. The garden was overgrown but there was a rose bush by the back door covered in flowers. Anna picked a single red rose and held it to her face enjoying its perfume. "With my share of the apartment sale I could make this into a lovely home," she thought. "Hmm, rent out the land, build a swimming pool, tennis courts and let rooms like Mrs Tyler, who had told her she was giving up her bed and breakfast business this year and going to live in France with her daughter.

Both women were lost in thought on their way back. Anna's head filled with ideas for a new life and Mrs Tyler thinking about a young woman, years ago, who had been George Adams' employee and had disappeared one night never to be seen again. Arriving home, as Mrs Tyler helped Anna from the car, she saw another car in the drive.

"Someone else wanting accommodation I'll be bound." No, not more customers. Mrs Tyler was surprised to see DS Walker sitting in the car.

"Hello, I just popped in to see how Mrs Hutchison was doing," he said getting out of the car. "We've found more remains in the barn so I'm back here. I shall be asking around the village for information regarding missing persons."

Mrs Tyler beamed. "Let's help Mrs Hutchison and then you come along in, I may have something for you."

Mrs Tyler watched as DS Walker gently helped Anna from the car. Hmm, methinks he held her just a bit too long, she thought as she hurried away to make some tea. With Anna settled in a chair DS Walker turned to Mrs Tyler.

"So you have something for me, Mrs Tyler?"

"Well, a few years ago there was a young woman working at Home Farm. Did a bit of cooking and housework but her main job was to look after the cows. Sturdy lass she was. Then one day, poof! She was gone, never seen again. George was a man of few words and never mentioned her other than to say she was gone and not coming back."

"And this would have been when, Mrs Tyler?" DS Walker asked.

"Now, let me see, our Brian got married around the time she went and his oldest is now nine. About ten years ago, I think. I always thought our Brian would take up with her. I know he liked her. Well, truth be told all the lads around here did. She used to drink pints in the pub with them and she was a good darts and skittles player. But then he went and married that stuck-up tart Stephanie. They got married sharpish. I thought she might have been in the family way but no, because our Kevin was born over a year later."

"Did you know her name?"

"Now, let me think… Yes, Jessie, that was her name, although George Adams always called her Jessica."

"Surname?"

"Can't help you there. I don't recall ever hearing it. Now, more tea anyone?"

"Has Mrs Tyler helped, Detective?" Anna asked as Mrs Tyler went off to make fresh tea.

"Well, we know the remains are female. We're waiting for further test results. But, yes, it could be of some help. I can ask around to see if anyone knew this Jessie's surname."

The next morning Anna asked Mrs Tyler if she could run her up to the farm again. During a rather sleepless night, Anna had had a thought. She had a key to the locked bureau in the living room at the farmhouse and fancied a peek inside. Mrs Tyler was more than happy to oblige as she was intrigued by the unfolding story.

Anna tried several keys before she found the right one to open the bureau. There were just a few old bills in the top desk area but the drawer below had letters and photographs. Anna looked briefly at the photos. They were of no one she knew. As she sorted through the letters she found one marked *To be opened in the event of my death, Signed G. Adams.* Anna quickly opened the envelope and started to read.

I am George Adams and I have a confession. I killed Jessica Toms. I didn't mean to do it, it was an accident. I asked her to marry me but she laughed in my face and told me she was expecting a babby and she wanted to marry the lad who was the father. Well, I kicked her out and told her to leave and never come back. She packed her bags and left. I didn't expect ever to see her again but one wet and windy night about six months later she appeared on my doorstep. Heavy with child she was. She was crying and asking to come in, had nowhere to go she said. She had hoped to marry the lad from the village but he had upped and married someone else. I told her she could stay the night but that's all. Later that night I heard her scream. She had started having the babby. I tried to help, having seen many cows give birth, but her screams got worse and I saw the babby was stuck. I just pulled until it came out. Poor little thing was blue, I rubbed it a few times but it was dead.

I told Jessica and she started beating and kicking at me I swung back at her and she fell and hit her head on the table next to the bed. One look at her and I knew she was a goner. Next morning I put the dead babby in a sack and hid it under the floor of the hayloft and buried the mother in the floor of the barn. I am sorry and may God forgive me.

George Adams

Anna was stunned. What a sad story, she thought. "Mrs Tyler," she called, "I have to contact that cop James Walker. I need to get back to your place."

Mrs Tyler came clattering down the stairs. "Found something, have you?"

"Yes, can we go please?"

A week later Anna was on her way to the airport after James Walker had offered to take her. "After all," he said, "you saved me a lot of time, finding old George's confession. The Super has decided we will close the case. Although I wonder which lad was the father?"

Anna had a pretty good idea. So did Mrs Tyler.

The Unicorn of Arne

By

Angie Simpkins

"Thanks, Mum," said Jenny, giving Margaret a peck on the cheek. "I know she'll be OK with you. She seems happier here, away from all the bustle of the town."

Jenny was talking about her daughter, Lucy, who was going to stay with her grandmother for a few weeks. Lucy was five years old, and six months ago had been in the car with her father when a juggernaut had pushed them off the road. They had ended up upside down in a ditch. Lucy's father was unconscious and Lucy, although unhurt, was upside down, trapped by the seatbelt, for some time until they were found. Fortunately her father, after a brief stay in hospital, made a full recovery but the shock and sheer terror felt by the little girl had caused her to lose the power of speech. She had been referred to several therapists, so far with no improvement. The doctors had advised Jenny and Peter that it was highly likely that Lucy would eventually make a full recovery, but they were unable to say how long this would take.

Lucy and her grandmother had always had a close, loving relationship, and Lucy loved the countryside and beaches that were close to Granny's home.

"Well, dear," said Granny as they went indoors. "I thought we might go to the beach this afternoon. It's a lovely day, we can paddle and build sandcastles."

Granny picked up the bag, which was already packed, and Lucy skipped happily out to the car. They spent several hours building a series of sandcastles, collecting pretty shells to decorate them, and Lucy ran up and down the beach, filling the buckets with water in a vain attempt to keep the moats full.

After tea and bath that evening Granny went to the bookshelf and picked out a book. "Look, Lucy, I have bought a new book, it looks really good. Shall we read it tonight?"

There was, of course, no reply, but Lucy snuggled up to Granny in happy anticipation. When Granny reached the end of the story about Percy, a magical and brave white unicorn, and Miranda, the beautiful princess, Lucy took the book and, opening it at the first page, handed it back to her grandmother.

"Do you like this story? Do you want me to read it again?" asked Granny.

Lucy nodded vigorously, but before Granny got to the end Lucy was asleep. This pattern was repeated every bedtime, the days being spent playing on the beach, or visiting Poole Park, feeding the swans or playing on the swings, slides and roundabouts.

As the weekend approached Granny said to Lucy, "Mummy and Daddy are coming to see us on Saturday. If the weather is nice, it would be good to take a picnic somewhere. What do you think?" Once again, she was answered by a nod.

On Friday morning they both went to the supermarket. Granny allowed Lucy to choose some items for their picnic – sausage rolls, crisps, chocolate biscuits. Granny then selected some more healthy additions, bread, cheese and fruit. On the way to the checkouts they passed through the clothing department. There, hanging on a rail, was a beautiful blue dress, just like the one worn by Miranda, the princess in the story. Lucy stopped and fingered the dress longingly.

"Oh my!" exclaimed Granny. "That is just like Miranda's dress, isn't it? I wonder if they have got your size," and she started to look along the rail.

"Yes, they have. Would you like it?"

Granny only had to look at Lucy's shining eyes to know that the answer was yes.

That afternoon Granny managed to persuade Lucy to change out of the dress for a few hours, and they once again spent a couple of hours on the beach. In bed on Friday evening Lucy, as usual, fell asleep while listening to the tale of the exploits of Percy and Miranda. In her dreams she was that beautiful princess, and the lovely blue dress lay on the chair beside her bed.

Saturday morning dawned. Lucy put her Miranda dress on as soon as she got out of bed. She went into Granny's room and stroked her face.

Granny woke with a start. "Oh, I thought for a moment that it was Miranda, and I was dreaming. You look just like her," and Lucy climbed into bed with Granny, handing her the book. "Just once then, this morning," said Granny. "We've got to prepare the picnic ready for when Mummy and Daddy arrive."

After breakfast they both set to work making sandwiches. Lucy put the things she had chosen in her backpack, and began to spread butter on the bread for Granny to make the sandwiches. Granny then made flasks of tea and filled a small bottle with orange squash for Lucy.

They had just finished when there was a ring at the door. Lucy ran to open it and there stood Mummy and Daddy.

"Well, how's my little princess?" cried Daddy, sweeping Lucy up into his arms. "You look like a real princess," said Mummy, putting her arms around Lucy too, and depositing a kiss on her head. "It looks as if you have been spoiling her, Mum. Why am I not surprised?" laughed Jenny.

Lucy ran out of the room and raced back in waving the book about Percy and Miranda.

"What an interesting looking book," said Jenny, kneeling down with her arm around Lucy. "You look just like the princess in the picture, doesn't she, Daddy?

"She certainly does," said Daddy. "What's the plan for today, Margaret? I'm sure you've made one!"

"Don't be cheeky, young man," came the answer. "In fact, it's a lovely day, I thought it would be nice to go to Arne. It's such a beautiful place, I know Jenny always loved going there, and since you approached middle age you have shown an interest in birds!"

"Touché," laughed Peter. "Arne it is then. Come on everybody, into the car."

Lucy happily skipped after her father, still clutching the precious book. As Jenny and her mother followed, Jenny asked, "How has she been Mum? Has she spoken?"

"Not a word," answered Margaret. "She is able to communicate well without words it seems. She just loves that book. I have to read it every night, twice, although she usually falls asleep before the end of the second telling."

After parking the car they headed for Shipstal Point.

"Just look at that view, and the heather," said Margaret.

"It's stunning," said Peter. "Who needs to queue in an airport and sit cramped in a plane for several hours, when this is on your doorstep? How lucky we are. Now, let's just find one of the hides and see if I can identify any of the birds, then perhaps we'll eat our lunch on the beach. What do you think, Lucy?"

Lucy nodded happily and ran along the path through the heather. They all sat in the hide and, while Granny and Mummy and Daddy looked for birds, Lucy took her book and, for the umpteenth time, looked avidly at all the illustrations.

When they got to the beach Mummy suggested that Lucy remove her dress so she could paddle, but as soon as she returned to the log they were sitting on, she had to put her dress back on. They all enjoyed the day so much that they were reluctant to go home and decided to explore more of the nature reserve. They set off across Coombe Heath and late in the afternoon saw many more birds come in to feed.

By the time they returned to the car park, most of the cars had left and a herd of deer was feeding very close to their car.

"Stand still," said Daddy, "don't startle them. We'll just stay here for a while and watch them."

"They are beautiful creatures," Granny said, and she sat down on a fallen tree to wait. Lucy sat next to her as they watched more deer arrive for their evening meal.

Suddenly, "It's Percy!" cried Lucy. "Look, Granny, it's Percy," and she leapt up in excitement.

Mummy, Daddy and Granny looked in amazement at the white stag that was feeding with the herd.

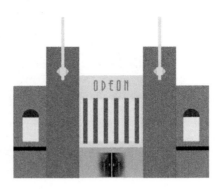

A Great Day Out

By

Shelagh O'Grady

Charlie reached the front door of Sunset Lodge retirement home with his friend Scottie in a wheelchair. They had planned a big day out and the two men were trying to leave unnoticed when Ralph appeared.

"Are you going out, Charlie?" he asked.

"We're going for a walk to get some fresh air," replied Charlie. "We won't be long."

"Can I come with you? I'd like a walk. Please let me come!" Charlie and Scottie exchanged glances.

"What do you think?" Charlie muttered to Scottie. "He may make a scene if we leave him."

"You decide, he's your friend," replied Scottie.

"Better bring him along, he'll be OK," said Charlie. He turned to Ralph. "You can come but stay close to me. I have to push the wheelchair, so no wandering off."

"Oh thank you, Charlie," beamed Ralph. "I'll do whatever you say. You're my best friend."

I just hope this works out, thought Charlie. Ralph held the door open as Charlie pushed Scottie outside. Before they could close it a voice called after them.

"Where are you three going?"

Charlie turned and saw Mollie, one of the care staff, watching them.

"We're going for a walk... er... to the end of the road. We may sit and watch the traffic for a while," replied Charlie, flustering a little.

"It's a nice day, so enjoy yourselves. Be back in time for lunch," she said, closing the door after them.

"That was close!" muttered Charlie as he pushed the wheelchair smartly down the drive.

"Aye, but she didn't stop us," replied Scottie. "That's a good start."

Having reached the bus stop on the main road the three elderly men sat in the sunshine, watching the traffic rush past. They looked a dishevelled bunch; Scottie's long legs looking awkward in the wheelchair with his red tartan tam o' shanter perched jauntily amid his straggling white hair. Charlie was wearing his ancient Harris Tweed jacket with leather elbow patches and his old cloth cap. Ralph looked scruffy in his crumpled trousers, faded patterned cardigan and blue velvet slippers.

"Is that yer slippers yer wearin'?" asked Scottie, peering at Ralph's blue velvet footwear. "Oh dear, yes it is," gasped Ralph. "I forgot to put my shoes on this morning! I'm sorry, oh dear, what shall I do?" he whined, panic rising in his voice.

"Don't worry Ralph, it's not a problem," soothed Charlie. "I expect they're comfortable, aren't they?"

"Oh yes, very comfortable. I like wearing them," replied Ralph forgetting his anxiety.

"That's fine, there's nothing to fret about," said Charlie. Scottie glanced at him, raised his eyebrows and shook his head.

Whilst watching the traffic, Charlie recalled how he and Scottie had planned this outing. Life at the retirement home in the leafy outskirts of Poole was very uneventful, so the two friends had decided to sneak into town one day and go to the pictures. Charlie had planned for just Scottie and himself, but with Ralph tagging along, Charlie hoped it would still work out.

As a bus drew into the stop, Charlie stood up and pushed the wheelchair towards it.

"Come on Ralph," he called. "We're going for a bus ride."

"I thought we were going for a walk," protested Ralph.

"We are, but we're going for a bus ride first," said Scottie. "You wanted to come with us, so on you get!" Ralph reluctantly climbed aboard and wandered down the bus whilst Charlie struggled with the wheelchair.

"Fares please," called the driver.

As Charlie and Scottie produced their bus passes Ralph began to look worried.

"I didn't bring mine with me, oh dear, what shall I do Charlie?" Ralph was near to tears.

"Have you got any money with you?" enquired Charlie. A quick search of his pockets produced a handkerchief and some empty sweet wrappers but no cash.

"Don't worry, I'll pay for you Ralph. Go and sit down."

Charlie handed over some coins and asked for a ticket to the town centre.

"Just wait til I'm settled before yer move this bus," Scottie shouted to the driver. Charlie secured the wheelchair and sat down. Scottie shouted again, "OK, on yer way now, but take it steady mind!"

The driver pulled away, muttering something under his breath.

"You shouldn't talk to the driver like that, Scottie," rebuked Charlie. "He could refuse to take us!"

"Aye, so he could. Maybe I'll just keep ma mouth shut for a wee while," replied Scottie, lapsing into silence.

Ralph gazed out of the window. "This is exciting," he exclaimed. "I haven't been on a bus for ages!"

"You enjoy the ride, Ralph. It's going to get even more exciting later on!" said Charlie.

Shortly after coming to live at Sunset Lodge, Ralph had made friends with Charlie, many years his senior. Although only in his early fifties, Ralph had been diagnosed with early onset dementia. His wife, feeling unable to cope, had placed him into care. She visited occasionally and Charlie got the impression that Ralph's condition did not suit her lifestyle.

"Dumped out of sight with us oldies, poor chap," thought Charlie. The simple, childish mannerisms which Ralph had developed as part of his illness appealed to Charlie's caring nature, and the two had become friends. Arriving at the bus station they got off and headed for the High Street.

"The town seems awfully busy today," said Scottie as throngs of shoppers and school children jostled past them on the busy street.

"Let's find somewhere quieter, maybe have a cup of coffee," suggested Charlie, anxious to get away from the bustling crowds. "Keep hold of my arm, Ralph," he said as they pushed through the crowds. "We don't want to lose you."

"There's too many people, I don't like it!" whined Ralph.

"Just keep holding on and you'll be OK," said Charlie. "Look, there's a fish and chip shop over there. Why don't we have some for lunch, I'm starting to feel hungry!"

"That's a grand idea!" replied Scottie. "Fish and chips would be just fine."

"Shouldn't we be going back for lunch?" worried Ralph anxiously.

"Ralph, today we have escaped from Sunset Lodge," explained Charlie. "Scottie and I planned this outing, and I'm afraid you've been caught up with it. We're going somewhere exciting today and we'll go back later, but not just now."

"What about my lunch?" wailed Ralph.

"Should hae left him behind," growled Scottie. "He'll spoil it all!"

"Don't be unkind Scottie," chided Charlie. "He's feeling a bit unsettled. Come on, let's get some lunch from that chip shop. You like fish and chips don't you, Ralph?"

"Oh yes! Yes I do," Ralph replied, his voice quaking a little. "My wife would never let me have them, she said they would make me fat. But I *do* like them!"

"That wife of yours sounds awfully dull," grunted Scottie.

"Come on chaps, it's lunch time," said Charlie hastily, sensing an argument brewing.

They entered the shop and joined a small queue. Gazing at the menu boards, they were staggered by the huge choice offered. Cod, haddock, scampi, sausages, pea fritters, piles of chips, the list was endless! Adorning the counter were jars containing pickled eggs, onions, gherkins, tomato sauce, brown sauce, barbeque sauce and various kinds of mustard. Frying smells hung enticingly in the humid air. When he had finished reading the menu Scottie muttered, "Will ye take a look at all that! I bet they havena' got a haggis to go with ma chips."

"If you ask I'm sure they could find you one," said an elderly lady standing in the queue. Scottie was a little taken aback as he had only been muttering to himself.

"Thanks," he replied. "Mebbe I will!"

"I'm going to have a large cod and chips," declared Charlie. "What about you, Ralph?"

"Oh dear," he whined. "Well, if you're sure we won't be going back for lunch, maybe I'll have the same."

"If ye don't have something to eat now, you'll be mighty hungry by the time we get back!" snorted Scottie.

"Charlie, I haven't got any money," Ralph wailed mournfully.

"Don't worry," sighed Charlie. "I'll pay for now. You can let me have it back later."

"Yes, gents, what can I get you?" asked the attractive young counter assistant, smiling at the friends.

"Would yer be having any haggis, ma bonny wee lassie?" asked Scottie. The girl turned and spoke to an older man who was dropping battered fish into the fryer.

"If you can wait I'll go and have a look. I think there might be some in the freezer," he replied. Scottie's eyes sparkled.

"That would be just fine!" he exclaimed.

Meanwhile Charlie placed an order for cod and chips twice, and the three friends waited, savouring the cooking smells. Soon the man returned with a dish in his hand.

"The last one, sir. I'll put it in the microwave, it won't take long."

A little while later the three men, each clutching a plastic bag, made their way to Poole Quay just a short distance away. Sitting on a bench in the sunshine they unwrapped their food.

"Whatever happened to good old fashioned newspaper?" sighed Scottie as he prised open the polystyrene box. "There's a wee sliver of wood in ma dinner!" he exclaimed indignantly.

"That's a fork," said Charlie. "Saves messing up your fingers."

"That's half the fun, eatin' it with yer fingers! There are too many new-fangled things these days!" Scottie muttered. Charlie helped Ralph to open his box.

"Are you sure it's all right to use my fingers?" enquired Ralph. "I usually eat my meals with a knife and fork!"

"We don't have any cutlery! Anyway, this is the best way to eat fish and chips. Try using that little wooden fork," said Charlie reassuringly. Scottie glanced over and raised his eyebrows but said nothing. They continued to eat their lunch whilst sitting in the sunshine watching all the activity on the quay and finished with cans of soft drink.

"That was a mighty fine meal!" exclaimed Scottie. "I haven't had anything that good in a long while!" He fumbled in his pocket, took out a pipe and started to smoke. "I'm startin' to enjoy myself now!" he sighed contentedly.

Ralph busied himself collecting the empty food containers and putting them in a nearby rubbish bin.

"Are we going back now?" he asked.

"Not yet," replied Charlie. "This afternoon we're going to the cinema." Ralph stared at him, open mouthed.

"Oh dear! Oh dear!" was all he could manage.

"We'd better get going. The cinema is back up the High Street," said Charlie. "Are you ready to go, Scottie?"

"Aye, I suppose I am. It's awful nice sitting here in the sun."

"Shall we leave you here?" asked Charlie with a chuckle.

"Don't you dare. I'm ready now," said Scottie, putting his pipe away.

Charlie pushed the wheelchair whilst Ralph kept close beside him. They threaded their way through the bustling crowds and soon arrived at the cinema.

"I don't remember it like this," said Scottie. "It's very fancy with all those lights and that posh carpet on the floor!"

"Things change, Scottie," said Charlie as they approached the ticket desk.

"Three pensioners' tickets, please," he requested.

"Which film do you want to see?" asked the assistant.

"What do you mean? How many films are you showing?"

"Six."

"Six! How can you show six films all at once?" asked Charlie in amazement.

"We have six screens in six separate theatres," replied the assistant patiently. "Now, which film do you wish to see?"

"We want to see the new James Bond film," answered Charlie, feeling a little awkward.

"You'll enjoy it. There's plenty of action and lots of pretty girls." She smiled and handed him the tickets. "The young man over there will show you where to go," she said, indicating her colleague. They were shown to their seats and soon had Charlie parked in a wheelchair space. As they settled down the adverts began, with sound levels high enough to cause them to wince.

"I don't like this. It's too noisy!" whined Ralph, clamping his hands over his ears.

"It'll be better when the film starts," shouted Charlie above the noise.

"This is grand," laughed Scottie. "I can hear everything, clear as a bell!"

Ralph gradually let go of his ears and Scottie and Charlie relaxed in their seats, mesmerised by the action. About halfway through the film Scottie decided he would like a smoke. Finding his pipe, he put it into his mouth, lit it and sat back. With clouds of smoke rising into the air, a ripple of angry voices buzzed around him.

As the air conditioning drew the smoke upwards things began to happen. The smoke detectors became activated and a wailing siren noise filled the cinema. Just as everyone started to leave their seats the sprinkler system sprang into action. Shouts and screams echoed round the auditorium as people were pushing and shoving trying to reach the exits, whilst others were jumping over the seats. Spilt popcorn crunched underfoot as frightened cinema goers stampeded for the doors. Water sprayed down unrelentingly, drenching everyone.

"What the hell's going on?" demanded Scottie. "I'm getting wet!"

Ralph began to cry. Charlie pulled him from his seat and grabbed the wheelchair. People were surging past in their rush to get out and Ralph was almost knocked over. Grabbing hold of him, Charlie pushed him to the front of the wheelchair.

"Scottie, let Ralph sit on your knees otherwise we will lose him in all this!" he shouted above the noise as he bundled Ralph on top of Scottie.

"My god, he's a great lump!" moaned Scottie, but he put his arms around Ralph and held onto him. Charlie tried to push the loaded chair through the surging throng but it was heavy and reluctant to move. Just as he was about to give up a tall, well-built man appeared out of the crowd.

"Here, let's give you a hand, Grandad," he said, taking the chair and pushing through the crowd. Charlie followed behind, very relieved that someone had come to their rescue. They followed the panicking crowds out through a fire exit and into a side alley. Once outside the tall man stopped and helped Ralph to the ground.

"Thank you so much!" said Charlie gratefully. "I was beginning to think that we wouldn't get out!"

"No problem. Glad to be of help," said the Good Samaritan as he disappeared into the crowd.

The three friends were a sorry sight, wet through and huddled together. Even Scottie was at a loss for something to say. Charlie looked along the alley towards the front of the building and saw fire engines and police vehicles blocking the road. As he waited two men in dark suits approached them.

"Excuse me gentlemen, would you come with us please?" said one of them.

"Who are you, where are you taking us?" demanded Scottie.

"I'm the manager of this cinema and this is my deputy. We would like to ask you a few questions. Gentlemen, this way please!" His tone was direct and uncompromising. The three bedraggled friends followed the manager with his deputy helping Charlie with the wheelchair.

"We're in big trouble now!" thought Charlie.

Much later that afternoon as the police van transporting the three friends arrived at Sunset Lodge, Scottie spoke quietly to Charlie.

"They weren't very happy with us at the cinema, nor at the police station, and I think we'll be in trouble again back here."

"We did seem to cause a bit of bother. Perhaps Matron will lock us in our rooms and throw away the keys," said Charlie with a half-hearted laugh.

"Well, whatever happens," said Scottie, "I'd just like to say this was the best day out I've had for ages, I've really enjoyed myself. Let's do it again sometime!"

Be Careful Who You Upset

By

Pam Corsie

Jacqueline stood in the mist and light rain at the top of the cliff at Dancing Ledge. She listened to the waves crashing on the pebbles 100 feet below and marvelled at how the vast wildness of the sea always helped her to get things into perspective. She looked back over her troubled life. It had started as an idyllic childhood living with Mummy and Daddy in the nearby cottage, but when mummy died it all started to go horribly wrong. Jacqui had been unceremoniously dumped from the pedestal Daddy had placed her on, by the wicked stepmother whom Daddy had married in indecent haste and whom had made Jacqui's life hell.

She was like two people: when he was at home she was the kind, attentive, smiley woman that Daddy had brought in to help take care of her; and a jealous, mean-spirited, spiteful harridan when he was not. Jacqui had been thumped regularly for every minor misdemeanour, constantly reminded of how useless she was at EVERYTHING and, worst of all, drip fed poison about how, since he'd remarried, Daddy didn't need her anymore. As wicked stepmothers went she was in a class of her own. No wonder Jacqui went off the rails.

Gradually, at first, she went from slightly stroppy, little bit sad but well-behaved young teenager to wild child. Eventually the wicked stepmother could no longer put up with her drug- and drink-fuelled antics. Even Daddy was losing patience and had stopped defending her. As soon as she reached 16 she was thrown out of the only home she had ever known. A home that had once been warm, welcoming and full of love, but now was a battlefield of immense proportions and deep sorrow. Daddy managed to stuff a small wad of notes into her hand before the wicked stepmother slammed the front door but that soon went on a bottle of vodka and some speed from the local dealer.

As the years passed by, Jacqui's life spiralled out of control and she found herself totally dependent on drink and drugs. She pole-danced in a Soho club by night, often taking clients to the private areas to earn the money she needed for a drug-induced sleep by day. When she was 24 Daddy came to find her. He'd been looking, without much success until now, since it had become obvious that she wasn't coming back of her own volition.

"I'm going through a sticky patch, Daddy. Usually I am having a great time, wild child extraordinaire, mixing with rock stars and the rich and famous. Anyway, what are you doing in a Soho club?"

"Looking for you. I've been looking for 8 years. Can we talk?"

"£50 will get you an hour in a private room where we can talk. Need to earn, Daddy, need to earn."

"I always thought wild children were into free living and didn't believe in earning money."

"Depends how wild."

They had talked for an hour then Jacqui had pushed Daddy out into the night with a promise to keep in touch. He was still married to that harpy, still living in the cottage on the cliff, so he understood she wouldn't be going back any time soon but they had swapped phone numbers and agreed on a weekly WhatsApp.

Jacqui learned through their regular messages that the wicked stepmother's health was failing. She had a ghastly muscle-wasting disease that meant she now spent a lot of time in a wheelchair. Daddy was doing his best to take care of her but he was still working full-time and Jacqui could read through the lines that the old cow was not the easiest of patients and Daddy was reaching the end of his tether.

It was four years since he had located her and he had been such a help. They'd kept in contact and he had arranged for Jacqui to go into rehab. She was doing well. Two and a half years sober and drug-free and she now had an NVQ in healthcare.

"And that's why I am here," she said out loud to no one in particular. There was no one else around on the misty cliff top covered in wild grasses where the seagulls swooped low and squawked in the hope of finding something to eat, even though the holidaymakers had long since gone back to their homes.

Jacqui pulled her jacket tightly around herself, turned and walked towards the cottage.

"Where have you been, you silly tart? You should have been here at ten," screeched the wicked stepmother.

"I'm not a tart," Jacqui replied patiently in the professional tones she used when addressing unpleasant patients. "Would you like a cup of tea?"

"You used to be a tart. Once a tart, always a tart. That's what I say."

"And you used to be a complete bitch and you still are," muttered Jacqui as she went to put the kettle on. She could feel the wild child in her surfacing. The wicked stepmother did this to her, more and more frequently, the longer Jacqui stayed in the cottage. The wild child in her had no boundaries and Jacqui was scared of what might happen.

She used a feeder cup to get the tea into her stepmother as she could no longer hold a mug on her own. "Would you like some fresh air now that the tea has gone?"

"No."

"I'm taking you outside anyway, fresh air is good for you."

"It's damp, I'll catch my death."

We can only hope, thought Jacqui. She pulled the shawl around the wicked stepmother's shoulders and walked along the pathway to the cliff edge.

"Look at that view. The mist has lifted. You can see for miles. The sea is beautiful. Enjoy, you old battle-axe."

As her stepmother turned as best she could to look at the so-called wild child who, until now, she had failed to goad to anger, Jacqui gave the wheelchair a sharp shove and sent it toppling over the cliff onto the pebbles about a hundred feet below. She heard the sea breaking on the shore and gobbling up her stepmother.

She got out her phone and WhatsApped Daddy. "I came to look in on her as usual today but there is no sign. Do you know where she could be?"

Saturn Runs Rings

By

Pam Sawyer

Ginny awoke at the sudden noise. She looked at the clock: 6.30. That flipping cat flap, she thought. She waited for the familiar padding of her cat's feet on the bare boards of the landing as he made his way into the bedroom and leapt onto the bed, purring loudly.

"Be quiet, Sats, it's Saturday. I need a lie in."

The cat soon settled beside her and they both slept.

Later, making her breakfast with the cat winding himself around her legs, Ginny's thoughts returned to a year ago. Edward, her late husband, disliked the cat. Edward was ex-army and terribly fussy about tidiness and said that a cat would make a mess. Ginny had never intended to have a cat but Saturn had appeared one morning on the doorstep and had refused to leave. Ginny advertised in the local paper and put notices on lampposts around the area but no one came forward to claim him.

The cat was here to stay, Ginny told Edward. He watched as the cat wound itself round Ginny's legs nearly tripping her up. She bent down and picked him up, stroking his soft fur. "That cat will run rings round you." Edward looked on in disgust.

"Rings, that's good," said Ginny. "I'll call him Saturn, Sats for short."

A few weeks later Ginny realised that Edward and Saturn didn't get on. What she didn't know was that Edward often kicked the cat or shoved him off the chairs or sofa. After Christmas the weather turned bitterly cold with snow and sharp frosts turning the roads and pavements icy. One morning when Edward left for work after Ginny, he wedged the cat flap on the door shut.

"Try getting back through that," Edward snarled at Saturn. The cat looked up at him and strolled down the path. Edward, now late for work, hurried down to the garden gate. He didn't see Saturn until the cat wound itself round his legs. Edward tripped and fell. Trying to regain his balance he landed in the road and was hit by a passing car. Ginny was at her office at the East Dorset District Council near Wimborne when she got the message to go to the hospital to see Edward. Sadly she was too late and he had passed away. Later that day Ginny was at home with Saturn on her lap. There was a ring at the door. Opening the door a police officer stood on the step.

"Mrs Ginny Mabey?" Ginny nodded.

"May I come in?" Ginny stepped to one side. "I'm police constable Don Jones. I'm sorry to hear of the tragic accident today. The driver of the car said there was nothing he could do, your husband seemed to stumble into the road."

"How is the car driver?"

"He's pretty cut up obviously."

"I feel so sorry for him."

"Yes, well there will be an inquest but it does seem to be an accident. How are you bearing up, Mrs Mabey? I see you have a companion." He pointed to Saturn. "Is there anything I can do? Would you like me to arrange for a family liaison officer to call?"

"No, thank you. I have got Sats for comfort."

Constable Jones started calling on Ginny using one pretext or another. Soon they started dating. Don didn't live with Ginny but he did stay overnight quite often. Early one morning Ginny and Don were asleep. Don was sprawled across Ginny, when suddenly Don awoke.

"What the...?" It was Saturn. He had jumped on Don's bare back, scratching him badly.

Ginny, now wide awake, asked, "What's going on?"

"It's that bloody cat. He scratched my back, look, he's drawn blood." Don struck out at the cat who hissed and jumped off the bed. "Look, he's left bloody footprints across the duvet."

If truth be told, Ginny was getting fed up with Don. He was rather demanding in the bedroom and although Edward was obsessed with tidiness, Don was the opposite, which was beginning to annoy the usually tolerant Ginny. She rose, had a shower and got ready for work. She fed Sats, had some breakfast and left Don asleep in bed. He wasn't due on duty until 2.00 p.m. Saturn was curled up on the windowsill asleep. Ginny dropped a kiss on the cat's head and left for work.

Ginny had a bad day at work, with loads of complaints from staff and customers. Her computer was playing up and she was looking forward to going home. Don wouldn't be there as he would be on duty. It would be just her and Sats and a large glass of wine.

There was a gentle knock on her office door. A female police officer entered.

"Mrs Mabey, Ginny?" Ginny nodded and stood. "Something wrong, officer?"

"I have some bad news I'm afraid." Ginny sat down. "I understand you and Constable Jones were, how shall I put it, close friends?"

"Yes, what do you mean were?"

"Constable Jones was involved in an RTC."

"RTC?"

"Sorry, road traffic collision. He was in his patrol car driving down your road when according to the colleague with him a large cat ran across the road. Don swerved to miss the cat and crashed into a lamppost."

"Oh my God. How is he?"

"He died at the scene."

Ginny burst into tears. "Poor Sats."

"Sats? Who is Sats?"

"My cat, Saturn."

"No, not the cat. Don Jones died at the scene. We have arranged for a council worker to check the lamppost and some of Don's colleagues have left flowers at the scene. Sadly it's right outside your house."

A couple of weeks later Ginny went to Don's funeral. She was greeted with sympathy by his fellow officers.

"How awful for you. First your husband and now your lover." Eleanor, the officer who had broken the news, put her arms round Ginny. Eleanor soon became a regular visitor at Ginny's. They enjoyed having a glass of wine together watching the same things on TV and Eleanor was an excellent cook. She always left the kitchen spick and span and often brought Sats little treats. Ginny had never been happier, finally breaking free from men.

One night Eleanor curled up in bed with Ginny, Sats purring gently at her side. Ginny was fast asleep. Men are so gullible, Eleanor thought. Keep your friends close and your enemies closer. She smiled as she stroked the contented cat.

The Airman

By

Angie Simpkins

He fought back the tears. He was a man, strong, a fighter. He shouldn't be longing for his mother now. Shivering, he began to drag himself along, detaching the straps of the parachute as he went. He attempted to gather it together, knowing that he should not allow it to be found, but his leg was so painful his first thought was to find shelter. He could see the flames from his burning plane about one mile away across fields. The soft rain was not enough to extinguish the flames, but more than enough to add to his discomfort.

The ground suddenly began to drop away beneath him. The sky was dark, no moon nor stars to be seen, but a gentle sound of slowly running water told him there was a stream nearby. He allowed himself to half roll and half crawl down the gently sloping bank until he reached the water. As he did so the clouds briefly parted and in the moonlight he saw a bridge, an old stone-built bridge carrying a narrow country road across the stream. He began to crawl towards the bridge and found that the water level was low and there was a narrow patch of dry sand under the bridge.

With relief he lay on the sand, sheltered from the rain and hidden from view. His eyes closed and he dreamt for a while. He awoke to the sound of his own voice – "Mutti, Mutti" – and on the realisation of his predicament he, once again, fought back tears.

He knew people would be searching for him; if only he had managed to hide the parachute. The dawn was breaking, perhaps he could manage to retrieve it before it was found and he began to drag himself back up the bank. When he reached the top he looked around. He saw a rural scene. It was unlike the familiar landscape of his home where his father's cattle grazed on meadows uninterrupted by forests and gentle hills like those he saw now surrounding fields of ripening corn bounded by hedges and woods. He also saw the sea, sparkling in the sun, but knew from his briefing that the steep cliffs of this part of Dorset would prevent him from reaching the shore. In the distance he saw men and horses and a very old looking tractor. Realising he would be unable to retrieve the parachute without being seen, he returned to his hiding place, deciding to make another attempt under cover of darkness, should it not be discovered before.

He lay back under the bridge, drifting in and out of sleep, still cold and shivering. The rain still fell but half-heartedly now, although it didn't ease the damp discomfort.

He sat up with a start when he heard voices. Children's voices. They were getting closer, and from the sound he knew they were scrambling down the bank. He took his pistol out of its holster and sat quietly waiting. Two boys appeared, they didn't look in his direction. He thought they must be about ten years old, and they began to dip small fishing nets in the stream. He sat in the shadow, as still and as quiet as a mouse, watching the boys.

"Tommy, Tommy, I've caught something," shouted the smaller boy excitedly. They reminded the airman of himself and his brother when they were young. He once again fought back tears as he thought of Jochen. The last time he had seen him Jochen was preparing to be sent to the Eastern Front. He put the gun away, knowing he would not be able to use it. The older boy, Tommy, stood and turned, catching sight of the figure under the bridge.

He was startled. "Who are you?" he spluttered.

"My name is Hans," answered the airman, attempting unsuccessfully to stand.

"That's a jerry name," cried the younger lad. "Tommy, Tommy, he's a jerry."

"I know that," said Tommy. "Go and get Dad and tell him. I'll stand guard."

As the youngster ran off as fast as his legs would carry him Hans looked at Tommy.

"You are a very brave young man," he said.

"I suppose you came from that plane that crashed yesterday," said Tommy. "We thought there were no survivors."

"I jumped out and parachuted down, some distance from the plane," said Hans, "but I'm afraid I have hurt my leg and could not walk far, and now I cannot walk at all."

"Well, you won't be walking anywhere for a while, PC Williams will lock you up until the Military Police come for you," said Tommy.

They sat in awkward silence for some time, it seemed an age to Tommy who didn't feel very brave, in fact, he was afraid and didn't know what he would do if Hans attempted to get away. It was with relief that he heard his father's voice calling him.

"Down here, Dad, under the bridge," answered Tommy and Hans watched as a strong, rough looking, weather-beaten man stumbled down the bank. "This is Hans, Dad," said Tommy, making a bizarre attempt at introducing the two men as if they were at a cricket match or a garden party. "He's hurt his leg."

His father surveyed the young airman. "You must have come from the plane that came down yesterday," he said, adding to himself silently, you don't look old enough to be flying a plane. "What's the matter with your leg, son?"

"I think it is broken, Sir," answered Hans.

"Tommy, go and get Bert and Fred, and tell them to bring old Henry and the cart," said the father. "I'll stay here with Hans and keep guard."

When Tommy had gone off to fetch the two labourers and the horse and cart Hans reached inside his jacket and pulled out his gun again.

"What do you want that for, son?" asked the boys' father. "Just how far do you think you'll get even if you shoot me? The nearest station is ten miles away, you could shoot me and Bert and Fred, but the Military Police would catch you long before you could escape – they'd probably set the dogs on you and I wouldn't wish that on anybody, not even a German."

"You are correct, Sir. I cannot shoot you. I do not think I could shoot anyone. I am not fit to be in the Luftwaffe," said Hans sadly, laying his gun on the ground.

The father picked up the gun, saying, "There are many young men who feel as you do. Don't dwell on it, lad, you will be spending the rest of the war in internment."

"I see where Tommy gets his bravery from," said Hans.

The father took from his jacket a pack of cigarettes, he lit two of them and passed one to Hans, who accepted gratefully and they sat there smoking in strangely companionable silence until they heard Tommy returning with two sturdy looking men.

"Mum's here too," said Tommy. "I told her that he'd hurt his leg."

The three men lifted Hans as carefully as they could, but he groaned as he was moved. They laid him on the flat floor of the cart and Tommy's mother gently felt his leg. He screamed as she straightened it, then tied it to a splint. She covered him with a blanket and sponged his forehead with a sweet-smelling cloth, "Danke, Mutti," mumbled Hans deliriously.

The journey back to the farmhouse was not easy, the roads were rough and the cart jolted and swayed. Hans was groaning most of the time. Tommy and his brother, Robbie, ran off to search for the parachute. They knew their mother and sister, Evie, who was going to marry her sweetheart when he was next home on leave, would be thrilled to get their hands on the silk.

The three men carried Hans into the house and undressed him surprisingly gently for three burly men. Annie, the farmer's wife, then sponged him with warm water, gently drying him too, until he had stopped shivering. She then spooned soup into his mouth. "Danke, danke," he said sleepily, and he fell asleep on the sofa, in front of the fire.

"Bert has gone to fetch PC Williams," Charles the farmer said to his wife.

"He can't be moved," said Annie. "He'll have to stay here until he can be moved to a hospital."

"Well, the Military Police will decide what's going to happen to him. We will not have a say in the matter," answered Charles.

It was not until the following day that the Military Police arrived. Hans was stronger by now, and was able to sit up, although he could not bear weight on his leg. The Military Police were not so gentle, but they did help him out to their transport and took him to the hospital in Wareham, where he was put in a side ward with a guard on the door.

Hans eventually made a good recovery, and after spending a year in an internment camp in the north of England, was trusted enough to be allowed to return to Dorset to do farm work as he did at home, and he spent the final two years of the war working for Charles and Annie, and teaching Tommy and Robbie to fish.

Entertaining the Visitors

By

Shelagh O'Grady

"Aren't you excited, Elmo?" drawled Thelma in her broad American accent. "We're going to look around a mansion, a real English country house! Imagine a sweeping staircase, grand rooms full of antique furniture, servants, titled people!"

"Yes, dear, it'll be wonderful," replied Elmo, not sharing his wife's excitement at visiting some crumbling English pile.

"Steady on, Aunt Thelma, there aren't any servants and the titled people are all dead. It's owned by the National Trust now," said Ben.

"I like to go visit these places and imagine myself living in all that grandeur. You have so much history here, a ruined castle, your Jurassic coast and now this old mansion. I'm in heaven!" Ella rolled her eyes at Aunt Thelma's American need for delving into English history.

Ben's great aunt and uncle were visiting from Palm Springs, Florida, doing a grand tour of the British Isles and were staying a few days at the prestigious Royal Bath Hotel in Bournemouth. Ben and his wife Ella had decided to take them out for the day and visit some local beauty spots. With everyone in the car, including Paddy, Ella's dog, they began in Sandbanks where they looked at luxury villas in "millionaires' row". Next they boarded the chain ferry to Studland and enjoyed coffee on the beach. After a stroll round Swanage they arrived at the Greyhound Inn in Corfe Castle village for lunch.

"This is where I like to go visiting," said Elmo smiling broadly, "a real English pub!"

"Such a pretty little village, quite charming," Thelma gushed as she peered into the village shops. "But those Roundheads made a real mess of the castle! Such a pity someone doesn't repair it!"

After driving through the scenic Dorset countryside Ben pulled into the carpark at Kingston Lacy, once the home of Lord and Lady Bankes. The beautiful old country mansion was set in acres of gardens and rolling parkland.

"Ben, you go round the house with Aunt Thelma and Uncle Elmo," said Ella. "I'll take Paddy for a walk. They don't allow dogs in the house." Paddy, the small brindle-coloured terrier was sniffing in the grass, glad to be out of the car.

"Can't think why you decided to bring that dog," said Thelma with thinly disguised dislike for the animal. "It should have stayed behind."

"Remember your manners, Thelma," grunted Elmo, "we're not at home now, dear."

"It would be too long to leave him at home," said Ella. "I've been round the house several times so I'm not missing anything." Thelma stomped off towards the entrance with Elmo scuttling behind.

"See you later, Ella," said Ben with a grin. "Enjoy your walk, Paddy."

"Glad she's your relative and not mine," laughed Ella.

Ben caught up with Thelma and Elmo at the entrance. "I've booked us onto a conducted tour of the house. They do one every day in the afternoon, and it's really good. You get to know so much more than just walking around and reading the guide book."

"That sounds fantastic!" said Thelma, snapping out of her huff. "Come on, I can't wait. I want to see all the beautiful things!"

They joined the small party for the conducted tour and set off around the house, Thelma hanging onto every word. The guide described the décor and the furniture and shared stories about past family members whose portraits were adorning the walls in many of the rooms. Thelma was intrigued by the tale of a ghostly lady sometimes seen standing on the stairs.

Ella was happy to let Ben spend time with his aunt and her long-suffering husband. Setting off she soon found an open grassy area where Paddy could run and chase his ball. Dotted around were clumps of trees surrounded by long grass and brambles. Ella managed to throw the ball into one of these grassy tangles and Paddy rushed after it, disappearing into the undergrowth. There was a loud yelp followed by muffled barking and he didn't return when Ella called him. Fighting her way through the brambles Ella found Paddy had fallen into a deep hole. She could hear him barking and peered into the darkness. Reaching for her mobile phone she switched on the torch and could see Paddy at the bottom of a shaft about ten feet down, seeming none the worse for his fall.

"OK, Paddy, there's no way you can jump out of there," said Ella. "I'll have to come down and rescue you." Noticing a set of wooden steps fixed to the side of the hole Ella decided to try them out. "They look a bit dodgy but here goes," she said to herself. Putting one foot onto the first step it appeared to hold her weight. As she started to climb down there was a soft, crunching sound and the slimy rotten steps collapsed. Paddy jumped out of the way as Ella landed on a pile of soft earth and leaves. Apart from being showered with earth and pieces of rotten wood she wasn't hurt. Paddy leapt over and licked her face.

"Glad to see you're OK, Paddy," said Ella as she pushed away the debris and stood up. "Next problem, how do we get out of here?"

Taking out her mobile phone Ella checked it for a signal but there was nothing. "We can't call anyone," she sighed, "and it's no good shouting. There was no one else around."

Ella peered around the space and found it was no bigger than a broom cupboard, dimly lit from the hole above. Using the torch in her phone she saw the steep, mossy walls gave her no chance of climbing out. The remains of the steps were hanging precariously, in imminent danger of collapse. Over one wall hung a curtain of roots and vegetation and when Ella pulled it to one side she found a wooden door. It looked as rotten as the steps and when she pushed, it collapsed. Peering inside she found what looked like the start of a tunnel.

"We might have discovered a secret passage, Paddy. Come on, let's see where it goes. It seems our only way out."

The tunnel was about six feet high with rough stone walls and a curved brick roof. Hanging from the brickwork were festoons of roots shining ghostly white in the torch light. Ella cringed as they brushed her face and stooped whilst trying to avoid them. The air smelt damp and musty and she was starting to feel claustrophobic. Glad of the light from her phone she picked her way carefully along the passage.

"Thank goodness I remembered to put my phone on charge last night," she thought as she stumbled over debris from a roof collapse and squelched through mud on the floor. Paddy kept close to her heels making no attempt to rush ahead. The tunnel twisted and turned and seemed to go on for a long time. Eventually Ella noticed that the roots had disappeared and the air smelt drier. Now spiders' webs hung everywhere and were sticking in her hair.

"Which is worse, roots or cobwebs?" Ella wondered, disgusted by the feel of both. The walls were looking drier and she wondered if they might be inside the house. Maybe we'll come out into the kitchen, she thought.

Presently she came to a set of stone steps leading upwards. Paddy climbed ahead and they found themselves in a narrow passage with wood panels lining the walls and ceiling. It was only just wide enough as her shoulders brushed each side. Ella stopped and listened, she could hear voices, faint and muffled but definitely voices. She sighed with relief hoping her ordeal would soon be over.

Quite suddenly the passage ended, widening slightly into a small room with a door set in the far wall. With mounting excitement she searched the door for a handle, having to work quickly as the light from her phone was starting to fade. Finding a large bolt she tried to pull it back but it fell off in a shower of rotten wood. Spluttering with the dust she groped around and found a large iron door handle with a substantial lock.

"Where's the key?" she asked herself in dismay. Ella searched around the walls and found a small recess. By the dim light from her phone she saw a large key on top of a book, both festooned in cobwebs. Gingerly brushing away the cobwebs she picked up the key and saw that the book was a Bible.

"That's an odd place to leave a Bible," she thought as she fitted the key into the lock, and struggled to get the ancient mechanism to work. Paddy was jumping around barking, sensing they would soon be free. Finally the key turned and as she pulled on the handle the door slowly swung open, the rusty hinges uttering a loud groan. Ella and Paddy stumbled through the doorway, blinded by the sudden brightness.

In the opulent drawing room the tour guide had been talking about the family portraits hung around the walls. Thelma was fascinated by ancestry and had asked lots of questions. As the guide started to describe the huge inglenook fireplace, a section of the wall slowly swung open allowing a small dog and a very dirty woman to stumble into the room. Ella stood open mouthed, blinking at her audience whilst Paddy shook the dust from himself.

A loud wail arose from the group and Thelma, still thinking of the ghost on the stairs, collapsed in a faint. Elmo and Ben turned to help her whilst the others stared in confusion. Paddy barked excitedly and ran over to Ben. Stepping over the rope barrier the guide approached Ella.

"I'm so sorry," gasped Ella. "Paddy fell down a hole in the grounds and when I went to rescue him, this was the only way out!" Dirt and dust fell from her clothes as she moved.

"My dear, are you alright? You look in a terrible state."

"I'm fine really, just a bit dirty and shaken up."

"You may have discovered a secret passage and the priests' hole. It's been known to exist for years but no one knew where it was."

"Oh really?" said Ella. "That's interesting."

"Let's get you cleaned up and listen to your story."

"I'm sorry, Paddy seems to have made a mess on the carpet."

"It's only dust. The cleaners can deal with that."

A room steward arrived with a blanket which the guide placed around Ella shoulders. "There, that will stop you shedding dust everywhere. Come with me, dear."

"My husband and friends are in your group. I think Aunt Thelma has fainted."

"The first aiders will see to her. This must be your husband," the guide continued as Ben approached with Paddy at his heels. "Let's get you cleaned up. I want to hear more of your story."

Following the guide Ella, Ben and Paddy were taken to the stewards' rest room. Ella was given some spare clothes to change into whilst the guide produced cups of tea and slices of Victoria sponge cake. Presently the door opened and Aunt Thelma and Uncle Elmo walked in.

"Are you feeling better, Auntie," asked Ella. "Come and sit down, we're being treated to tea and delicious cake."

"Thank you, dear. How are you?" asked Thelma sinking into a chair, her face still shocked and pale. "You gave us quite a surprise when you appeared in the fireplace. I thought you were a ghost!" After a good laugh Ella told her story.

"The Trustees will be very interested in this," said the guide. "They will want to speak to you later."

"Ella, my dear," drawled Aunt Thelma, "thank you so much for a really exciting day. I'll have so much to tell my friends when we get home!"

"She'll dine out on this for a long time!" sighed Uncle Elmo. "Years probably!"

A Faint Whiff of Old Pipe Smoker

By

Pam Corsie

"It has potential," said Terry, trying to inject some enthusiasm into his voice.

"It also has some sort of fungi growing on the kitchen walls, a cracked, original, stone sink, a soggy, wooden draining-board, a walk-in pantry, picture rails and a bathroom circa the late 1940s: the last time the place saw a paint brush, I should think," grumbled Sarah.

"It would make a lovely family home with a bit of imagination and a lot of hard work," Terry persisted.

"It also has nicotine-stained, floral wallpaper, ragged nets, inch-thick dust, cobwebs like fishing nets and more than a faint whiff of an old pipe smoker!"

Terry and Sarah wandered out into the overgrown garden with their three children, who were quite excited at such a large space to play in. Lurking at the bottom of a huge stretch of twelve feet long brambles, waist-high grass and a crumbling, broken brick path was a dilapidated shed. Sarah dragged on the rickety door and it came away in her hand, any traces of functioning well-oiled hinges a long forgotten luxury.

In one corner was an upholstered, reclining chair that looked as though it had provided lunch and bedding for several vermin, a wonky side table, battery radio and piles of paperback books. It was the well-used pipe in the ashtray and tortoiseshell spectacles, with one cracked lens, that brought a lump to her throat. The house might make a lovely family home but, it appeared, the previous owner was more comfortable in the shed.

"Cooee, dear. Helloooo! Can I help you?" came a voice from the other side of the overgrown hedge. Sarah and Terry glanced at each other with raised eyebrows. This could make or break the deal. They'd resigned themselves to having to take on a mammoth DIY project if they were ever to afford their own place. But, after they had spent all that time, money and energy making it comfortable, they were hoping for some privacy to enjoy their family and didn't want to be bothered by nosey neighbours.

"Are you thinking of buying?" she asked. Then, without waiting for an answer, "It would be lovely to have a family living next door. I'd enjoy hearing laughter and conversation again after all these years."

"After all what years?" Sarah asked, deftly fending off a kick in the ankle from Terry that warned, don't encourage her.

"Well, my dear, I've lived in Hazelbury Bryan all my life and my mother and father before me. I'm Vera, by the way. The next door neighbours have always lived there too, until they died, of course. His mum and dad were friends with my mum and dad. We were friends too when we were children, me and Archie. But he wasn't the same after the War."

"I think a lot of people were very different after the War," Sarah commented. She was far too young to know first-hand anything about the War or its implications on returning men and women, but felt she should join in the conversation. Not that her prospective neighbour needed any encouragement.

"He was stationed overseas, you know. Army. Not injured when he came home, well nothing you could see. Just changed. Didn't talk to anyone. Got a job as a plumber's mate. In fact, his first job when he came home was to put a bathroom upstairs for his mum and dad. When he wasn't working, he mainly sat in the shed with his books."

"They're still there," said Sarah.

"When his mum and dad died I thought he'd spend more time in the house as it was all his to enjoy. But no, I don't think he slept there but, especially after he retired, he spent most of his time in the shed, reading and listening to the wireless, always with a pipe in his mouth."

Well, that would account for the general decay surrounding the place and the faint whiff of old pipe smoker, Sarah thought. The neighbour was unstoppable and Sarah wondered if she and Terry were the first people Vera had spoken to in a long while.

"Don't know what made him be like that," the neighbour mused. "He always looked so sad, unfulfilled somehow. And yet his mum made him lovely meals and looked after him properly when he came home. He just didn't seem able to move on with his life."

"Such a shame," Sarah replied, somewhat inadequately. The children were racing around in the undergrowth, snagging their clothes on vicious brambles, playing a game of tag, oblivious to the scruffy state of their surroundings and thoroughly enjoying the space. Space was at a premium for a family of five living in a two-bedroom flat. This awful garden and uncared-for house could be just what they needed.

"So, dear, what do you think? Are we going to be neighbours? Are you and your family going to give this old girl some conversation and laughter to listen to over the fence?"

"Do you know, Mrs... ?"

"Wilson. But, please call me Vera."

"Do you know, Mrs Wilson, er Vera, I think we just might. It's a lot of hard work and loads of money, but it sounds to me as though this house needs more than just an injection of practical things. I think it needs love and we can give it that."

Terry glanced at Sarah, the look on his face one of complete amazement that his practical wife would have such a romantic opinion on what she had been, up until now, describing as a ghastly pile of cracked bricks and dirt.

"Come on, carry me over the threshold," Sarah teased.

"Are you kidding? I've got a lot of work to do here. Most of which I won't be able to manage with a hernia," smiled Terry.

Vera Wilson laughed. "How wonderful, I'm laughing already and you've not moved in yet."

After the tortuous process of completing the purchase they finally had the keys and, bravely, Terry carried Sarah over the threshold again and then had to go back three times for each of the children, who didn't understand the significance of being carried over the threshold, but didn't want to miss out.

They were going to live with Sarah's parents while they made the house habitable, which was a relief for them, if not for her mum and dad! Their main objectives were to make the electrics and plumbing safe and working, install a new kitchen and bathroom and then they felt they would probably have outstayed their welcome at mum and dad's and ought to move in and decorate the other rooms as and when they had the time and could afford it.

They had to do a lot of the work themselves and get professionals in for the difficult bits. This meant, of course, that the work Sarah and Terry did mostly consisted of destroying and demolishing the inside of the house. Making it a lot worse before it got better. Mrs Wilson was a delight, supplying coffee, tea and homemade cake and biscuits a couple of times a day at the weekends, encouraging them to keep going and make the family home ready for the neighbours she longed for.

She also hung around a bit too often on occasion – nothing is perfect – and asked lots of questions about things they may have found while removing old furniture, ripping up floorboards and tearing down wallpaper. She was determined to get to the bottom of the mystery of Archie's inability to get on with his life and thought the answer might be hiding somewhere in the house.

The water was turned off, the chipped and crazed basin from the bathroom languished in the skip in the front garden next to the ceiling-high cistern with the clanking chain and the stained, white loo marked TJ Crapper, the name for a toilet manufacturer their oldest daughter found hilarious. The bath was making its way down the stairs like a cape on Terry's back, thudding on each step and he was grunting along with each thud. Sarah looked at the stripped, empty room and felt a bit sad as it dawned on her that they had erased the only bit of Archie's handiwork in the house.

A floorboard wobbled beneath her foot. Nothing unusual in that as all the floorboards wobbled, so she didn't know why this particular wobble captured her interest. She gently levered it up and, hiding amongst the debris of the long ago plumbing job, was a wallet, cracked, brown leather, mould growing on it now and looking well worn. As she opened it she felt as though she was trespassing. Three one pound notes, so it had been there a long time. What's this? A letter! She was really feeling the angst of an eavesdropper now but couldn't stop herself.

My dearest Archie,

By the time you read this you will be home, in your de-mob suit, three pounds of back wages in your wallet, settling back in with your mum and dad. From what you've said about them I know they will look after you which is why I feel I can write this letter. We are no longer hundreds of miles away from people who know and accept us, we can no longer behave in a way that pleases us but would offend everyone who loves us. So I am saying farewell to you, to our love and any possible happiness we might have managed in between all the probable upsets.

I will never forget you, with all my love, Cyril x x

And therein lay the mystery of Archie's life. Mrs Wilson was right about this house holding Archie's secret. And here it will always stay, Sarah thought, as she replaced the wallet and carefully nailed down the wobbly floorboard.

We would all like to show you how we can work together. We collaborated on the following script for a radio play which was great fun but also required a certain amount of tact and understanding. We got there in the end!

<u>GO GIRLS</u>

By

Pam Corsie

Shelagh O'Grady

Pam Sawyer

Angie Simpkins

<u>SCENE 1</u>

<u>LARGE COUNTRY HOUSE IN THE DORSET COUNTRYSIDE, FAMILY HOME OF RETIRED COLONEL GEORGE MONTGOMERY-SMYTHE, THE LADY ELIZABETH AND THEIR THREE ADULT CHILDREN, EDWARD, SON AND HEIR, DOROTHEA AND CUTHBERT. THE YEAR IS 1913. THE DAUGHTER OF THE HOUSE HAS JUST RETURNED FROM TIME SPENT WITH AN AUNT IN SOUTHAMPTON.</u>

<u>DOORBELL RINGS, SITTING ROOM DOOR OPENS AND CLOSES</u>

ELIZABETH: Ah, Dorothea, you're home. Do come in, dear. Sit down. I've rung for tea. Mrs Brown is on her way. Tell me, dear, how did you find Southampton and Aunt Polly?

DOROTHEA: Southampton was interesting, Aunt Polly was well, Mama, and she sent you her best regards.

ELIZABETH: Did you go to the ball, dear? I want to hear all about it. Was that nice young man, Reginald, there? The nephew of Viscount Albarn, I believe?

DOROTHEA: Yes, Mama. The ball was wonderful and Reginald was there. I danced with him three times and also with two friends from his regiment.

<u>SITTING ROOM DOOR OPENS. GEORGE ENTERS</u>

GEORGE: Dorothea, whatever were you thinking of? Is this true? Constable Hobson says you set fire to the Royal Mail.

ELIZABETH: She did what? I don't believe it.

DOROTHEA: Yes, it is true. I did it in support of my fellow suffragettes.

GEORGE: Fellow suffragettes? Never heard such nonsense. You are not to have anything to do with that rabble. I shall have to

106

thank Hobson for bringing you home. He says on this occasion he will take no further action.

<u>SITTING ROOM DOOR CLOSES. GEORGE LEAVES</u>

ELIZABETH: What have you been up to now, child?

DOROTHEA: Cousin Jessica has become close with two old school friends. The day after the ball we all joined the NUWSS pilgrimage to London.

ELIZABETH: You went on a pilgrimage?

DOROTHEA: Not a religious pilgrimage, Mama.

ELIZABETH: Is there another kind and what do all those letters mean?

DOROTHEA: The National Union of Women's Suffrage Societies. Lots of women marched from all over the country, including Southampton, but we caught the train up and joined them when they reached the city. We walked into Hyde Park with them. Everyone was cheering and waving flags. It was so exciting.

ELIZABETH: That was very unwise. Not the sort of behaviour I would expect of you.

DOROTHEA: I've told Jessica that I will go back with her again. So Papa and you will just have to get used to the idea. I really believe in this cause. It's only fair that women should be able to decide what is happening in this country and have some control over their own lives.

<u>SITTING ROOM DOOR OPENS. GEORGE ENTERS</u>

GEORGE: How did you get involved with that lot?

ELIZABETH: It was Jessica's fault, she took Dorothea to a rally.

GEORGE: Do you mean the Suffragette Rally? I've been reading about them in the Times. Irresponsible women stirring up trouble for themselves and everyone else. They should be at home looking after their men folk.

DOROTHEA: Papa! I think they're very brave.

GEORGE: Brave? Huh, what do you know about them?

DOROTHEA: I was there, Papa, in Hyde Park. That's how I know about them and their mission. Their enthusiasm was so infectious. So liberating.

GEORGE: What? You were there? Does Aunt Polly know? I will have a word with Henry. He surely doesn't allow his daughter to behave in such an unladylike manner. Elizabeth! Speak to your daughter.

DOROTHEA: Oh, Papa!

DOROTHEA FLOUNCES OUT OF ROOM SLAMMING DOOR

ELIZABETH: Calm down dear, she's only young.

GEORGE: She's not young, she's 21 and should be married and settled down not gallivanting to London and spending time with miscreants. She's always been headstrong, she needs taking in hand.

DOOR OPENS AND CUTHBERT ENTERS ROOM

Ah Bertie, wouldn't you agree?

CUTHBERT: I might if I had heard the beginning of the conversation. Anyway, what's up with Dotty, Pa? She's stamped upstairs, slamming doors and now I can hear her crying in her room.

GEORGE: Bertie, do you know anything about this nonsense about votes for women?

CUTHBERT: No, but old Freddie Ginsberg's mama is mixed up with it, much to his old man's disgust. Still Mrs G's not the sort to mess with, is she? I keep out of it. So, Dotty has got herself involved has she? What do you think Mama?

ELIZABETH: Well ...

GEORGE: Your mother will have nothing to do with it. Isn't that right, Elizabeth?

ELIZABETH: Er, no, whatever you say, George.

GEORGE: That's right, my dear, that girl should be concentrating on getting a husband. That would take her mind off this rubbish. Votes for women, indeed! Bertie, have you seen anything of Edward today?

CUTHBERT: Yes, he's supping cider with the peasants, down at Home Farm.

ELIZABETH: Cuthbert!

GEORGE: Bertie, stop that. The Carvers are a very hardworking family and are making a good job of that farm. It would do you good to remember that people like them help to keep you in the style to which you are accustomed. Let's have some manners please.

CUTHBERT: Sorry Mama, Papa.

SCENE 2

IN THE DRAWING ROOM OF THE HOUSE

ELIZABETH: George, dear, how long do you think this war will go on for? I can't stop worrying about Edward, out there fighting the Germans. I keep praying for his safe return.

GEORGE: He's doing a great job defending the country. We can't have Fritz walking all over us, old girl. If only Cuthbert was as industrious as his brother. Edward understands the running of the estate and has gained the tenants' trust. They seem to be running rings around Bertie.

ELIZABETH: He's hopeless, isn't he, much as it pains me to admit it? Dorothea would have made a much better job of it. If only she had been born a boy.

GEORGE: She's never here. Always charging about the countryside, supporting those damn women. They may have put a brake on their vandalism during the war but Dorothea is as enthusiastic as ever.

ELIZABETH: I rather hoped she would have tired of it by now but she hasn't. I'm impressed by her tenacity.

GEORGE: Elizabeth! Whatever next?

DOOR OPENS AND CLOSES

GEORGE: I'll take that, Mrs Brown, thank you.

ELIZABETH: Oh George, a telegram, oh no.

SCENE 3

IN THE DRAWING ROOM AFTER THE WAKE

ELIZABETH: It was comforting to see so many at Edward's memorial service, darling.

GEORGE: Good of Captain Jenkins to speak so eloquently about Edward. Damn fine fellow. Cuthbert, you are going to have mend your ways as the estate will now be all yours one day. You will have to run it and make a profit. No slacking.

DOROTHEA: Why should it be Cuthbert? I'm the next eldest after dear Edward. I talk with Mr Carver about the farm and we have discussions about things like finding new horses, managing without them and what crops to grow. I know far more about running the estate than Cuthbert, who knows absolutely nothing about any of it.

GEORGE: You've been wonderful Dorothea when you're not sneaking off to attend those wretched meetings with those ghastly women. They, and you, should be at home looking after things.

DOROTHEA: Women are no longer "at home" all day. They are keeping the wheels of industry turning whilst the men are away fighting. Young Milly, Mrs Brown's granddaughter, is working on the buses in Dorchester as a conductress.

GEORGE: They are working class, my dear. Ladies in your position don't go out to work. It's just not done!

DOROTHEA: Papa, things are changing. Women of all classes want to work. After this dreadful war is over, women who have done the men's work in industry will not want to stay at home. Working makes them feel valued and respected. It gives them a feeling of independence.

GEORGE: Don't lecture me, Dorothea. I don't know where all your ideas come from. When this war is over everything will go back to being the same as before.

DOROTHEA: No, Papa, it won't! The Suffragette Movement will make certain of that. Whilst we are not so militant under the present circumstances we are as determined as ever. You won't be able to turn back the clock. Things will never be the same!

GEORGE: Dorothea, I don't like your attitude. If this continues I won't allow you to have anything more to do with those Suffragette women.

DOROTHEA: Papa, you can't stop me! I'll do as I please. I believe in the cause and I'm going to help change these outdated attitudes. There's a big rally in London at the weekend. I'm going to meet Jessica there.

GEORGE: I forbid you to go.

ELIZABETH: Dorothea, dear, do be careful.

DOROTHEA: I am going! Don't worry, Mama. Now, I'm off to Home Farm to thank everyone for coming to Edward's service.

DOOR SLAMS. DOROTHEA LEAVES THE ROOM

GEORGE: She's a wilful, headstrong woman. I need a brandy!

DOOR SLAMS GEORGE LEAVES THE ROOM

ELIZABETH: (LOW) I think she's really rather brave.

SCENE 4

IN THE SITTING ROOM

ELIZABETH: I miss Cuthbert so much since he was conscripted. He's been gone for almost eighteen months and not a word. I worry that he may not come back safely.

GEORGE: We all do, dear, miss him and hope that he returns in one piece. Only sorry I couldn't go myself!

ELIZABETH: You did your bit at Mafeking, darling, and lost an arm and half a leg for your trouble. I couldn't bear it if anything happened to Bertie, especially after losing Edward. I seem to have spent my whole life worrying about men.

DOROTHEA: Perhaps they're not so good at running things as they think they are, Mama.

GEORGE: That's enough of that sort of talk, Dorothea. The Representation of the People Bill is going through parliament right now. Isn't that enough?

DOROTHEA: Not enough, Papa, but a jolly good start. Mrs Pankhurst says ...

GEORGE: I don't want to hear a word that that woman has uttered. It's all absolute balderdash.

ELIZABETH: Do you think so, dear? I've been reading some of her speeches in the Times, she seems awfully well informed.

DOROTHEA: Mama, are you my latest recruit?

GEORGE: No, she is not.

ELIZABETH: You have others?

DOROTHEA: Milly, of course, and several of her fellow clippies. Dorchester is becoming a hot bed of revolutionary girls and women.

GEORGE: Undermining the structure of society. No good will come of it. You mark my words. Votes for women, indeed. What do they know about anything?

ELIZABETH: Probably a lot more than our generation gives them credit for, George. After all, your own daughter has done a wonderful job running the estate since Cuthbert went to fight. With your invaluable help of course!

GEORGE: Yes, well ...

ELIZABETH: And the tenants all think she is marvellous.

DOROTHEA: Thank you for saying so, Mama. I'm really enjoying it. I feel as though I am doing my bit to help the war effort. Mr Carver and I have doubled the size of vegetable producing acreage, we are feeding the whole village.

GEORGE: Yes, well, I suppose that was one of your hair-brained schemes that happened to have worked.

ELIZABETH: George, darling, give the girl some credit.

KNOCK AT THE DOOR

ELIZABETH: Come in, Mrs Brown. What is it?

MRS BROWN: Letter for Miss Dorothea, Ma'am.

DOROTHEA: Oh, who can be writing to me

TEARING SOUND OF ENVELOPE BEING OPENED

It's from Freddie, Cuthbert's friend.

ELIZABETH: Oh no, I can't bear it.

DOROTHEA: It's alright, Mama. Cuthbert's not dead. But he is in a field hospital. Freddie says he will be sent back to Blighty when he is well enough to travel. He was caught up in a mustard gas attack. He asked Freddie to let us know, Mama. He can't write himself. He can't see and his breathing is difficult. He says the Army will let you know when he is to be repatriated.

SCENE 5

IN THE SITTING ROOM

SINGLE RING AS TELEPHONE IS REPLACED

GEORGE: Dorothea, my dear, I have just had a telephone call from Bertie's CO, splendid chap, knew him in South Africa. He's pulled a few strings and he has managed to get Bertie transferred to a convalescent home in Dorset. I suggested to your mother that you and I should visit him first. You have seen how she is. Totally overcome, so I think it would be best for us to see Bertie and report back. What do you say?

DOROTHEA: Certainly, Papa, whenever you wish.

GEORGE: As soon as I hear he's been moved we'll make our plans.

SCENE 6

CONVALESCENT HOME

FOOTSTEPS ON GRAVEL, DOORBELL RINGS, DOOR OPENS

GEORGE: Ah nurse, we are here to see my son, Bertie. Cuthbert Montgomery-Smythe, recently arrived I believe.

NURSE: Yes sir, come with me. Have you been advised of his condition?

GEORGE: Dose of mustard gas I have been told.

NURSE: A bit more serious than that, I'm afraid. Ah, here we are. Lieutenant Montgomery-Smythe, your father and sister are here to see you.

GEORGE: Bertie, my boy, how the devil are you?

CUTHBERT: Well, apart from not being able to breathe properly and unable to see a damn thing, I suppose I am fine. Dotty, so kind of you to visit. Are you sure you can spare the time? I've heard from old Freddie what a splendid job you're making of running the estate. What's an old cripple like me supposed to do?

GEORGE: Now, now, Bertie. Don't get all worked up, it's not going to help your recovery.

CUTHBERT: What recovery, Pa? I'm a mess.

DOROTHEA: Things are bound to improve when we get you back home. Back in your old room you will feel so much better.

CUTHBERT: Hah, my old room, how do you expect me to get upstairs? Grow wings and fly? I am confined to a wheelchair, you know.

GEORGE: (LOW) Dorothea, my dear, I think we should leave. We don't want to tire the boy.

CUTHBERT: Pa! I can't see. I'm not bloody deaf!

GEORGE: Language, Cuthbert! There are ladies present.

CUTHBERT: I wish I could see them.

SCENE 7

IN THE BREAKFAST ROOM

CROCKERY RATTLING, RUSTLING OF NEWSPAPER AS GEORGE READS

GEORGE: I see in the Times today that Parliament has passed the Representation of the People Act. Women have the vote!

ELIZABETH: Oh, that's good news. Dorothea and her friends will be pleased. Such progress.

GEORGE: Balderdash! Anyway, we've got enough trouble with Bertie being so badly affected by mustard gas. I spoke to Dr Appleyard yesterday and he said there wasn't much chance of any further improvements. It looks as though Bertie will not be able to run the estate on his own, even if he had the inclination.

ELIZABETH: George! Bertie can't help his condition. He's terribly depressed about it all.

GEORGE: Sorry old girl, but I had such plans for him and this damned war has upset everything.

ELIZABETH: Dorothea has done a wonderful job whilst Bertie has been away. Mr Carver speaks very highly of her. I think you should let her continue, if she is agreeable.

GEORGE: I don't like leaving things in Dorothea's hands, however efficient she might be. It's not a woman's job.

ELIZABETH: There you go again, George. Everything has to be a man's job. Surely if Dorothea is capable and willing that's enough?

SCENE 8

IN THE DRAWING ROOM

DOOR OPENS, CREAKING WHEELCHAIR TRUNDLING, DOOR CLOSES

DOROTHEA: Hello Bertie, how are you today? You still look a little peaky. Do you feel strong enough to come down to the village? Jack Carver is here delivering vegetables to the kitchen. I am sure he would push you in your chair.

CUTHBERT: I will not go out in this thing, wrapped up like a baby or an old man. I can't bear for people to see me like this.

ELIZABETH: Hush, dear, don't upset yourself. Take your time. I'm sure in a few weeks you will be back to normal.

CUTHBERT: Mama, I will never be normal again. I envy Edward, at least he didn't have to put up with all this.

ELIZABETH: Cuthbert, that's a dreadful thing to say. My poor Edward.

SOUND OF WEEPING

DOROTHEA: Now look what you've done, Bertie. You've upset Mama.

DOOR OPENS

GEORGE: Have you seen this? Now look what your friends have done, Dorothea, and those fools in Parliament.

DOROTHEA: What, Papa? What is it? Let me see - oh, that's wonderful news. Women can finally use their vote, at least those over the age of 30. Well, I suppose that's a start. The fight must go on until all women have the same rights to vote as men.

GEORGE: Are you alright, Elizabeth? You look a bit upset. It's not going to make any difference to us. I'll tell you who to vote for. Now, Bertie, old chap, would you like to come to my study? We need to go over the accounts.

CUTHBERT: How can I, Pa? I can't see and I just feel so terribly weak. It's all I can do to hold a glass to my lips. Speaking of which, Dotty, be a dear and fetch me a port and brandy, would you?

GEORGE: The answer, Cuthbert, does not lie in alcohol. If you wish to take over the estate you are going to have to learn

114

how to do so with your disabilities. Do you think it's been easy for me for the last eighteen years?

DOROTHEA: I'll look at the accounts with you. I know what Jim Carver needs for the farm and I think we may need more help in the house, perhaps someone to help Mama take care of Bertie until he is stronger.

GEORGE: Very well then, come along Dorothea. It looks as if I am going to have to get used to this new world. We'll be ruled by women before we know it.

DOOR CLOSES

Acknowledgements

Shelagh, Pam S, Pam C and Angie would like to thank their families once again for their support and encouragement during the writing and production of this anthology. We would also like to thank the thousands of readers of Ladies in Beach Huts, our first anthology, who gave us the confidence to carry on writing and produce another. And, once again, we would like to express our gratitude to Karen of KS Editing. She has proofread our work and been of notable support and encouragement for another year.

We are delighted to have inspired Isabel, Angie's granddaughter, who wrote her own story using maps and reference books to place it in Dorset. A marvellous piece of work for a 10 year old and we are honoured to include it.

Angie, Pam S and Shelagh would like to express their thanks to Pam C whose enthusiasm, energy and hard work has made this project actually happen.

Printed in Great Britain
by Amazon

80455859R00068